IN DREAMS

LACYNDA MATHES

World Castle Publishing, LLC
Pensacola, Florida
Copyright © 2025 Lacynda Mathes
Hardback ISBN: 9798262139408
Paperback ISBN: 9798891264618
eBook ISBN: 9798891264625
First Edition World Castle Publishing, LLC, September 29, 2025
http://www.worldcastlepublishing.com

Cover: Cover Designs by Karen
Editor: Karen Fuller

Dedicated in loving memory to my mother, Demitra Siadys Murphy.

I miss you every day.

September 19, 1943 – May 13, 2003

PROLOGUE

Dover-Foxcroft, Maine
July, 2009

Gideon Spencer grabbed his abdomen as he doubled over in pain.

"Am I dying?" he wailed.

"You'll be alright, Sweetheart," his mother comforted him.

"That'll teach ya to eat potato salad out of a hunting cabin fridge," his older brother Issac scoffed. Isaac had turned 15 in March, and he thought he was an adult...at least as compared to Gideon, who had turned 13 yesterday, when he'd eaten the offending potato salad on a dare from 17-year-old Steve Unger. Scott, Steve's younger brother, had warned Gideon that Steve was not to be trusted, and Gideon fully believed him, but Steve had still managed to goad him into it. Issac had caught them just as Gideon had swallowed the last bite. He had proceeded to beat Steve up. That hadn't prevented the full twenty-four hours of hell that Gideon embarked upon about 20 minutes later.

He couldn't keep anything down. The pain was excruciating. He was sweaty but cold. No matter what his mother said, he was fairly certain he was dying.

Thankfully, he lost consciousness as his mother hit a pothole.

At least he was pretty sure he had lost consciousness,

because he was no longer in the backseat of the Ford Explorer his mother drove. He was out at Greeleys Landing, sitting on a red and white gingham blanket, like the one his mother used for picnics. He was looking out over Sebec Lake. A girl's voice broke the silence.

"Who are you?" she said. She was sitting on the blanket beside him. Had she been there all along, or had she just materialized as she spoke? He wasn't certain. She was a pretty little thing, though…maybe not as old as him, but she was already budding. She had a sweet, heart-shaped face, a pink, naturally bowed, full mouth, almond-shaped eyes that were a striking sapphire blue, and long, curly black hair. She appeared to be at least partially Asian, despite the sapphire eyes and curls.

"Ahhh, Gid…dion," he stammered.

"Hi Deon. I'm Tracey," she smiled. "Do you know where we are?"

"Sebec Lake," he replied.

She nodded. "I've never heard of it, but it's pretty here. I'm sick. I fell on a broken bottle, and it got infected," she explained, pointing to a bandage on her arm.

"I'm sick, too. I ate old potato salad on a dare," he replied.

He didn't care that he was sick anymore. He sat and talked to Tracey, perfectly contented. They spent an entire afternoon together. He told her how he had a crappy birthday. She wished for a cake, and it appeared on the blanket.

He made a wish and blew out the candles before sneaking a quick kiss.

She blushed adorably.

Then, he heard a beeping sound piercing the

dreamscape. She sighed, slipped the friendship bracelet she was wearing off her wrist, and laid it in the palm of his hand. "To remember me by," she said as she started to fade.

"I don't have anything for you," he protested, but she had vanished into thin air, and he was alone by the lake.

————

Richmond, Virginia
May, 2019

Tracey pulled the blanket up over her and turned off the bedside lamp. That date had been one of the worst she'd ever been on. Ernie...his name was Ernie, for God's sake... Ernie was late picking her up. He chewed with his mouth open. He farmer-blew his nose as they left the restaurant. She had made an excuse of having an early meeting in the morning and had taken an Uber home.

Home...such that it was...was a nice enough apartment. But she had no real home, no family. Her father had died when she was a baby. Her mother had died in a car crash 5 years before, right after her 18th birthday. She had been unable to keep the apartment they had shared when she went away to school in Blacksburg, and when she had returned to Richmond, that place was long gone, not that it had been home, either. She and her mother had lived a somewhat nomadic lifestyle. She'd lived in this apartment for 6 months now. Her furniture was functional, and the walls were still blank.

She wondered briefly if she'd dream of him, *her dream guy*, again tonight. She had met a boy a few days before her mother's accident, while visiting colleges in Boston with her tech-minded classmates and guidance counselor. He had been the student guide for her tour of MIT. And she had developed a massive crush on him in the blink of an eye. She had hung out with him the rest of the day…just to be near him…to the point where she nearly missed her bus home because she had lost track of time. It had been a chance encounter. They hadn't even exchanged information. But for the last 5 years, she had dreamt of him regularly. They were lucid dreams, where the two of them met on a grassy spot on the shore of some strange lake. They would sit and talk all night…well, day, in the dream.

In the last dream, he had told her he was getting married, her subconscious telling her it was time to let go and find a real boyfriend, no doubt. After the date she'd just suffered through, she was hoping her subconscious would allow her to experience the fantasy a little longer.

Sure enough, she drifted off to sleep and found herself sitting on a gingham blanket beside the lake. Her heart soared as he approached.

"Hi there, Tracey," her dream guy said, sitting next to her.

"Hi, Gideon," she replied, happy to see him, though he looked dejected.

"My fiancée took off. She left me and our daughter. I really thought she would help me accept that you aren't real, but instead, here I am, coming to you because she's gone."

"Or because I can only find horrible men with disgusting habits, and I can't let go of the perfect guy I've dreamt up," she quipped. They both laughed.

"So, we both claim to be the real person doing the dreaming," he chuckled. "Whatever, I'm just happy to see you again, Tracey. I had a crap day. And whether I am dreaming you, or you are dreaming me, you're my best friend."

CHAPTER 1

Piscataquis County, Maine
September, 2025

Tracey Hyun rolled down the window. Her heart had jumped into her throat when the strange man had knocked. The rain was coming down in torrents, and the man was huddled under the jacket he had removed to hold over his head, causing his face to be cloaked in shadow, like some grim reaper in a horror movie. The windshield wipers slapped and beat out a rhythm in concert with the rain. Then she saw the badge on his chest and the gun on his belt. With deep relief, she noted he was a Piscataquis County Deputy.

"Are you okay, Miss?" the man asked, yelling over the pouring rain.

"Yes. Thank you. I'm just waiting for the rain to slow down. Is that okay, Officer?" she answered.

"You'd be more comfortable if you came inside the store," the deputy yelled over the storm. "It's dark out here… and there have been some disappearances along this stretch of road over the last year. Three separate women, all traveling alone…all on rainy nights, like this," he said.

Tracey raised the window, grabbing her purse and umbrella. She exited her old Impala and opened the umbrella, running for the door of the convenience store she had parked outside of a few miles outside the Dover-Foxcroft town limits.

Once inside, she shook the water off the umbrella and

turned to look at the deputy. He was in his 30s, with dark hair and a dark mustache. He had an olive complexion and a distinct New Jersey accent. She smiled. "Thanks, Deputy…?" She looked at his nameplate. "Moretti."

He did not smile. He merely grunted and made his way to the coffee counter.

She was suddenly aware that the clerk and the deputy were staring at her. She closed the umbrella and greeted the clerk. "Hi. I hope it's okay to wait in here for the rain to slow. I can't see the road in front of me."

"Oh, sure, Honey. You want some coffee while you wait?" the clerk, a woman in her late fifties, with a plump figure and long brown hair pulled back in a low ponytail, asked her. Her accent was heavy with that Maine twang. Tracey chuckled, imagining the woman saying, "Ye can't get there from here." It was a joke she was beginning to understand, having found herself at the end of a long road after a wrong turn earlier in the day. You literally had to go back to get anywhere.

Tracey dug into her pockets. "How much is it? I need enough cash for breakfast in the morning. I'm traveling on a budget," she laughed.

"Oh, no charge, Honey," the clerk laughed. "Not on a night like this."

Behind her, the bell on the door rang as someone came into the store. "Dang," the man swore. "It's not fit for man nor beast out there tonight." He laughed. His good nature bubbled over, in direct contrast to the dour mood of the deputy.

Tracey turned to look at the newcomer. Her legs nearly went out from under her.

Gideon, the real-life Gideon, smiled, and her breath

caught. God, he was gorgeous. How was it possible that he looked exactly like he did in her dreams? He was tall, at least 6'1", with sandy blond hair and blue eyes. He had a square jaw, a straight nose, and an absolutely perfect mouth. Tracey opened her mouth to speak, but nothing came out.

He looked up from under his hat and into Tracey's blue eyes, a striking feature on her Asian face. His mouth dropped open, and they stared at each other long enough that the clerk cleared her throat.

"Gideon?" Tracey squeaked out. He took a step towards her and reached out, taking her by the elbow.

"Tracey?" he gasped. His puzzled expression matched her feelings as the two of them stood there staring at each other.

After a long pause while she tried to wrap her mind around it, she said, "Oh. Yes. I'm Tracey Hyun. We met… well, 9 or 10 years ago now, I guess. How are you?"

"Um…Good," he answered, looking like he was trying to wrap his head around something, too. "And…you?" he asked, releasing his grasp on her arm.

"Good. I guess. Confused. Sorry. Um…you live around here? And you're a deputy?" She pointed out his uniform.

"Oh. Um…Yes. I live around here. And I'm a deputy," he repeated back to her.

Deputy Moretti scowled and hung his wet jacket on the back of a chair. In the dark, his features had been obscured. In the light of the store, he was quite handsome, but his demeanor was gruff, and he wasn't especially approachable.

As for the real-life Gideon, Tracey honestly thought he was the most handsome man she'd ever laid eyes on. He was the polar opposite of Moretti. His smile reached all the way into his eyes.

The clerk cleared her throat again. "You want that coffee?" she offered, pouring Tracey a cup. "How do you like it?"

"Just two Splenda, please," Tracey said, smiling warmly. "Thank you so much."

"Where are you headed?" the clerk asked, handing her the cup.

"Goose Fields Farm. My mother grew up there. I'm heading out to my grandparents'. They recently passed away, and I'm the only remaining heir," she said in a fake English accent, laughing.

"Your mother?" the clerk asked. "Are you Judith Ford's daughter?"

"Yes, Ma'am. Did you know my mother?" Tracey asked, sitting at the table, pushing her jet-black hair back behind her ears.

"Sure did. She was my best friend in school. My name is Gretchen Banks, and this here is Deputy Gideon Spencer, um…but it seems you've met before. And the sour puss there is Deputy Dominic Moretti."

"I'm Tracey. Tracey Hyun. Nice to meet you," she replied, offering her hand to the clerk, who shook it.

Gideon nodded and smiled again. "Nice to meet you again, Miss Hyun. I'm at your service." Did he swallow hard? He bowed at the waist, one hand behind his back. The other, he twirled from his head out in front of him, using his own fake English accent. He straightened and flashed a charming, rakish grin, offering his hand. Dom sighed derisively and poured himself a cup of coffee from one of the two pots on an orange Formica countertop in the corner.

Dom walked over to the table and took a seat across from Tracey. "You travelling alone? You should be careful, Ms. Hyun," he grumbled.

Tracey smiled. "You're certainly less scary in the light, Deputy. Out there, I kinda thought you were a Jeoseung Saja," she laughed.

"Oh, just call him Dom, and I'm Gideon. You know…" His voice trailed off. "I mean…What's a…Sashoon Sasha?" he asked, good-naturedly, butchering the pronunciation. He sat in the chair next to Dom.

"Um…Jeoseung Saja…A Korean Grim Reaper," she said, tilting her head enigmatically.

"Oh. Wow," Gideon chuckled. "How is that different from an American Grim Reaper?"

Dom scowled again and shook his head, apparently in disbelief.

"Well, no scythe," she answered. "And a Korean Grim Reaper wears a honbok and a wide-brimmed black hat, not a cloak. Also, there's more than one…*a* Jeoseung Saja, not *the* Grim Reaper. They're bureaucrats who help guide the departed into the afterlife."

"Ah, I see," Gideon added.

Was she awake? This certainly wasn't the lake. And she could feel the chair under her rear end. She could smell and taste the coffee.

"So, you're…South Korean?" he asked.

"Hmmm. Biologically, half. My father was from Seoul. But I never knew him. I grew up in Richmond, Virginia. I'm pure American," Tracey answered, taking a sip of the coffee. It was good and hot with just the right boost of caffeine. "My knowledge of Korean culture is purely academic." She chuckled again.

"And fueled by K-Dramas," they said in unison. Holy crap! She'd talked to him about K-Dramas in her dreams. What was going on?

He laughed nervously. It was a great laugh, full, originating from deep in his chest, reflected in his eyes. "I'm just plain American. English descent…"

"All the way back to the Mayflower," they said in unison again.

"Hey…me too…on my mother's side anyway," Tracey laughed. "I'm sorry. I have déjà vu big time."

"Ayuh…me too," he muttered.

"Hmmm?" she queried, leaning forward.

"Nothing," he replied quickly.

"Italian, 3rd generation American. My great grandparents were from Naples," Dom interjected, looking back and forth at each of them.

"I would have guessed that," Tracey said, smiling, as Dom's mood slowly improved with each sip of his coffee.

The truth was, the rain was kind of freaking her out. It had been in her dream, too, along with the Jeoseung Saja… or serial killer…or moth man…or whatever that had been in her dream after Gideon had left. The thing was, it wasn't the first time she'd had that dream, either, the scary one. She was 27 years old, 28 next month, and she had dreamt that same dream at least once before, when she was 18, just before her mother died in a car crash, on a rainy, dark night, on a country road, in rural Virginia.

Her age was important. At least, it was according to the old woman in the tea shop in Koreatown in Los Angeles, when Tracey had visited the neighborhood last October while in Los Angeles for the Future of Business Technology and Communications Conference. The old woman told her that as of January 1st, she would really be 29…even though she wouldn't turn 28 until November 26…and so the coming year, this year now, would be her "a-hop-su", an age of probable misfortune. She had looked into the superstition and learned that the Korean age used to be 1 year at birth and increased by a year on January 1st, regardless of date of birth…so someone born on December 31, for example, would be 2 years old on January 1st, despite being born the day before. So, her mother would have died when she was 19 in her Korean age. Nine was considered an incomplete number and, therefore, unlucky.

She honestly didn't believe in superstitious nonsense like that, but looking at a man she'd been dreaming about for nearly a decade had her questioning that disbelief. Also, on January 3, she had unexpectedly been laid off from her job as a network administrator, which she had held since graduating from Virginia Tech 5 years prior, despite having just been sent to the conference in Los Angeles in October. Kingsford Technology Systems had acquired the company she worked for, and her job had been made redundant. She had to admit, 2025 had started out on a sour note. And she had been going through her savings and unemployment benefits ever since. It was late September now. She was nearly out of money and had not yet found a job.

But then she'd gotten a letter from Francis Hancock, Esquire, advising her of her inheritance in Maine. She'd never known her grandparents and had honestly thought they had died before she was born. It was a surprise to learn they had passed away in May and June of 2024, and that they had left everything to her. That at least seemed a stroke of good luck, as with no job and little savings left, she wasn't going to be able to afford her rent next month. She had taken what meager funds she had and packed as much as she could into the Impala, selling whatever she couldn't to her friends to bolster her travel budget. She had headed off to the wilds of Maine.

The wilds of Maine. That was fairly accurate. Piscataquis County was by and far the most rural county in Maine, with only around 16,000 residents. The county seat of Dover-Foxcroft, the town she'd left just as the rain had started, was home to approximately a quarter of the county's population at around 4,200. Her farm was approximately 8 miles away, out in the middle of the county, but with the rain, the dark, the mountains, and her not ever having been here before, she was reticent to travel the short distance. So, she had pulled into the convenience store's dark parking lot to at least wait out the downpour.

That's how she found herself staring at the literal man of her dreams. Somehow, looking at his smile, hearing his full, deep laugh, it didn't feel like an incomplete year anymore, Korean Grim Reaper haunting her dreams notwithstanding. Having recovered from the initial shock, she sat and chatted with him. It was easy and flirty, just like in her dreams.

As the rain began to slow, she checked her watch. No way was the lawyer still going to be at the cottage. She sighed. Hopefully, he'd followed through with getting the electricity and water turned on.

"You said that 3 women have disappeared out here over the last year?" she asked, thanking God she'd had the good sense to pull over when the rain had become so heavy.

"Mmmmm. Ayuh. People are understandably very

concerned. They've disappeared somewhere between Peaks Kenny Lodge and Greeleys Landing," Gideon replied.

"All three of their cars were located at Greeleys Landing. I think they all made it there," Dom added.

"Dom believes they were suicides," Gideon said, sadly. "And there was no evidence of anybody else being there. There were no other tire prints in the mud...rainy nights remember. But there were no footprints at all. So, unless they teleported, I'm not sure jumping into the lake explains their disappearances, either."

"I just don't think we're dealing with a serial killer," Dom added. "I don't mean that my suggestion explained away everything. But they were all in pretty desperate circumstances. Hailey Burns had split with her husband and was on the verge of losing custody to him. Grace Kemp had been depressed for years, had attempted suicide at least two times prior, and Becky Hawk was about to be charged with embezzling $3,000,000 from the bank where she was VP."

"All true," Gideon agreed. "I'd just like some evidence either way before I decide which it is."

Tracey had to admit her own circumstances were pretty desperate. What if she disappeared? Would someone just assume she had killed herself? She was even more glad she'd decided to come inside the little convenience store.

Eventually, the rain slowed to a drizzle and then stopped.

"I'll lead you out to Goose Fields Farm, if you like," Gideon offered. It's just a few miles, but it's down a dirt lane off the main road, so it's kinda hard to find, especially in the dark."

"You wouldn't mind?" Tracey asked.

"Nah. No biggie. I live at Drake Vale Farm, down the same lane," he laughed. "We're neighbors."

CHAPTER 2

George Byron Davison, age 55, was quietly contemplating retirement as he lowered himself into his desk chair at the Maine State Police Barracks at 2360 Congress Street in Portland. He felt old watching the troopers today. He'd been with Troop G of the Maine State Police for 22 years now, after 10 years with the Portland Police Department. After days like this, that seemed like a lot of years. His back felt every one of them.

They'd worked with the DEA, MDEA, and border patrol to intercept a major fentanyl shipment that had crossed into Maine from Canada. It had been a long f'ing day.

"Sergeant Davison," Trooper Trent Forrest greeted him. "That was what I call a great day." The young man sounded so incredibly self-satisfied that George had to smile.

"I'm glad you found that invigorating. I found it exhausting," he chuckled.

They had spent hours directing traffic around the car carrier as agents searched each vehicle and the truck. The haul had certainly been worth it, but directing traffic was hardly what George had signed up for. He had been the youngest officer to make detective with the Portland Police Department. Being relegated to traffic duty, while certainly necessary, felt demeaning. Especially when it started raining...and then pouring.

He was tired. Bone tired. At one point, at around noon,

he could have sworn he saw Shawn's old Impala. God, he missed his old partner. They had been as close as brothers. Shawn was the best of them. And he had loved that old '69 Impala. He'd spent hours polishing its shiny black paint job on his days off. Then he'd gone and gotten killed in the line of duty, leaving behind his family: a wife, a kid, and a sister... George's wife.

Maybe it was seeing a vehicle so like his brother-in-law's that had soured his mood.

It certainly had brought up all those same feelings of watching Shawn get shot and watching his best friend die in front of him. He had insisted on being the one to tell Shawn's wife. He may as well have shot her, too. She had collapsed and required hospitalization upon hearing the news. It had been the worst day of all their lives. It scarred them all.

The Lieutenant laid a firm hand on George's shoulder, causing him to jump. He hadn't noticed his approaching. "Good job today, Gentlemen. I promise you will get the next juicy case that comes in, George. Don't be discouraged."

"I'm not really. Just wet and tired," George replied good-naturedly. "After a hot meal and a good night's sleep, I'll be right as...rain." He winked. The three men laughed, not because it was funny so much as because they were comfortable with each other...because it relieved the stress of the day...and they needed to laugh.

It was enough to remind George that he loved his job and the officers he worked with. He wouldn't put in for retirement just yet. He had a feeling he had more to do.

———

Gideon led the pretty young woman down the dirt lane, past his own trailer on his parents' farm, past the Christmas tree farm he owned with his brother Isaac, to the small sheep farm she had inherited. The house was a small cottage, built in the late 18th century, one of the oldest structures in the area. Isaac had been caring for the livestock since the Fords' passings and was hopeful that the new owner would sell him the sheep and grazing rights. Having met the girl, Gideon was inclined to believe that she might do just that. She didn't strike him as a farmer.

Her grandparents had modernized the home and had recently updated the kitchen and bathroom, so while the home was old, it was comfortable. He helped her inside with her bags and the few boxes she had packed in her car and showed her around quickly.

She smiled brightly and shook his hand again at the door, her face resplendent in the soft glow of the porch light. Gosh, she's just as cute as in my dreams, he thought, as he walked carefully back through the muddy yard to his cruiser. She was tall for a Korean girl, but given she was only half Korean, that wasn't all that surprising. Her looks were a strange blend of exotic Asian and American girl next door. Though she had the jet-black hair of an Asian, it was curly. She had several little freckles across her pert nose. She had almond-shaped eyes, but the irises were a deep sapphire blue. And her complexion was a creamy ivory. Her lips were full and pink…and a little pouty. Her face was a sweetheart shape. Everything about her appearance was pleasing to the eye, at least his eye, anyway.

How was she here? How was she real? He knew she existed, obviously. They had met before, but the real girl was just a distant memory, and a stranger where the dream girl had become a part of his psyche. This girl…the one he'd just been flirting with, was the dream girl without a doubt. There had been things he couldn't explain…but they still had always happened in his sleep. He was fully awake this time.

She was still standing in the doorway when he reached the cruiser, so he smiled and waved as he climbed inside. He'd left her with his number in case she needed anything. He honestly hoped she'd need something.

He didn't say anything about the dreams. What could he say? "Hey, I have lucid dreams about you." How nuts would he sound? It was already nuts that he'd called out her name and grabbed onto her like some kind of crazed stalker.

He started the engine and backed slowly out of the muddy drive into the muddy lane, pulling away, careful not to spin out in the muck.

———

Tracey felt the silence. It was overwhelming.

The cottage was comfortable. The lawyer had gotten the electricity turned on. She'd tested the sink, and she had running water. There was even working cable…supplied by Unger Communications, the cable company that seemed to hold a monopoly in New England. But she was absolutely alone in the house, and she was miles from anywhere…alone.

She shifted nervously in the queen-size bed. She'd taken a bath to warm up after the rain. The down duvet was cozy…but she was uncomfortable.

Her phone chirped, and she jumped at the first sound since the running water an hour before. The caller ID read "Gigi." She laughed at herself and picked up the phone.

"Hey, Geege!" she greeted her longtime best friend. She tried to sound cheerful, and Gigi heard the effort in her voice.

"You okay, Trace? You need to come home?" her friend asked earnestly.

"No...I'll be okay. I'm used to living alone. I've just never been quite this alone...I mean, it's a nice house, but it's miles from anyone," Tracey chuckled.

She wanted to tell Gigi about Gideon, but her dreams about the handsome man were the one thing she never shared with her best friend. They were hers, and hers alone. And even if she had shared them, Gigi was very grounded. She'd never believe that the man Tracey dreamt of was real. She'd tell her that she had created the persona she dreamt of and was projecting that onto the real man. Tracey didn't want to hear that right now. She wanted to hold onto the dream. She wanted Gideon to be the Gideon of her dreams.

So, she sighed and decided to reminisce with Gigi instead.

"Hey, you remember that camping trip after I got out of the hospital?" she reminded her friend. "I feel kind of like that."

"Oh, yeah. Sure, I do. We went to Sky-Line Drive. It was beautiful. But it rained so hard that first night," Gigi said, laughing.

"Yeah, it's raining now...and boy did it pour earlier," Tracey laughed.

"Hmmm. I made you that friendship bracelet that night...because you lost the one I made for you at the hospital."

"Hey! I don't know what happened to it. I woke up from my fever, and it was gone. But I still have the one from the camping trip." She looked down at her wrist at the faded thread bracelet. "I'm wearing it now," she advised her friend.

"I know, Babe, but you moved to frickin' Maine. I

have to tease you, or I'll miss you too damn much," Gigi said, sniffing.

"I'll miss you, too, Geege. But I want to give this place a chance. It's not like Virginia had all that much to offer me... aside from you, of course."

"Of course," Gigi agreed. "I'm the best."

"You absolutely are," Tracey agreed wholeheartedly.

It started to rain again as Gideon ran from the cruiser into his trailer. Sphinx, his gray tabby, jumped onto the counter as he opened his fridge, taking out the milk jug and drinking from it, before replacing it. "Hey, Sphinx," he said, lifting the cat, giving him a pat before depositing him back onto the kitchen floor. "Hungry?" He opened a cabinet and took out a can of cat food. He opened it and dumped it in the cat's food bowl. Then he took the water bowl and filled it at the kitchen sink. "I just met my future wife," he said, replacing the water bowl and rubbing the cat from his ears down his spine to the tip of his tail. "She moved here, just like she told me she was doing in my dream last night. Now all I need is an excuse to ask her out," he laughed.

He took out his phone, sat on the sofa, and turned on his television. "Hey, Mom," he said into it. "I'm home. Is Cassie asleep? It's kind of a sucky night. Think she could stay with you tonight? Thanks, Mom. Ayuh, I'm a little late tonight. It was raining really hard, and I met the Fords' granddaughter at the Stop Buy. Dom and I kept her company until the rain stopped, then I showed her the way to Goose Fields and helped her into the house with her things. Ayuh, she's nice. Ayuh. She's pretty, too." He laughed. He couldn't hide anything from his mother. She saw right through him...

always.

After he talked to his mother, he showered and dressed for bed. He shut off his light and snuggled down into his bed. He wondered if he'd dream about Tracey again. Maybe he could ask her what the heck was going on in a dream. It wouldn't sound nuts in a dream. So, with Tracey on his mind, he drifted off to sleep.

He wasn't exactly sure what a hanbok was, but he pictured a Neo/Matrix type long black trench coat and a Kung Fu type hat, and that is what the Jeoseung Saja wore in his nightmare. The monster's face was obscured in shadow, but the hands were a horrible white pallor, with long skinny fingers, not bone, but certainly bony. The thing walked along Greeleys Landing shoreline. As a car approached, the creature raised its chin, releasing the lower half of its face from the dark shadows, revealing deathly white cheeks and jawline, and a deep, blood-red mouth. It reached out its grotesquely pale hand and crooked its talon-like finger, motioning for the driver of the approaching vehicle to come to it. A woman in a long flowing white dress…a wedding gown perhaps…emerged from the car and walked slowly toward the monster as the wind whipped around her, blowing the skirt and her dark hair wildly around her, covering her face. She reached out for the monster, and he opened his arms to her, enveloping her in the shadows swirling around him like her skirt around her as they both sank into the lake. As they disappeared beneath the dark water, Tracey Hyun appeared beside Gideon, slipping her trembling hand into his. "Did you see it, Gideon? Did you see the Jeoseung Saja? Ohhhhh," she moaned. "Who was she?"

"Christine. She was Christine. My daughter's mother.

She left me 4 years ago…when Cassie was just a month old," he answered sadly. "Did that thing kill my girlfriend?" he asked.

"No," Tracey answered. "He just took her to the afterlife. Somebody else killed her. This isn't nearly so nice as our conversations."

He slept dreamlessly but fitfully for the rest of the night and awoke more tired than when he'd gone to bed when his mother pounded on his door. He opened the door to find her looking worried and harried. "Oh, Honey!" she exclaimed, grabbing him by both arms. "They found Christine's body…at least they think it's her. The body washed ashore at Greeleys Landing last night in the storm."

CHAPTER 3

Gideon, off duty and dressed in plain clothes, approached the police tape around the area near the boat ramp at Greeleys Landing. His hands were stuffed inside his pockets.

It was an unusually warm morning in late September. The rain and wind from the night before had whipped up Sebec Lake. The long-submerged body of a young woman tightly wrapped in black trash bags with duct tape and weighed down by something that finally broke loose from the tattered rope tied around the grotesque bundle was discovered on the shore under a large spruce by a Cub Scout pack on an early morning hike.

Gideon's heart was breaking all over again. Was it really Christine? Had he spent the last 4 years hating her for leaving Cassie and him when she was…wrapped up like that in garbage bags with duct tape? He closed his eyes, and a sob escaped when he felt the warm touch of a consoling hand on his elbow.

He opened his eyes to see Tracey staring up at him with sad sapphire blue eyes. It felt so familiar. She was exactly who she always was in every single dream, a comforting presence, the best friend he'd ever had, his confidante, the woman he longed for. His lip quivered, and his eyes filled with tears. Tracey said nothing. She just slipped her arms around his neck and hugged him.

Gideon Spencer found himself clinging to the woman as he cried on her shoulder. When he had cried himself out, she released him and offered him a tissue. He laughed suddenly, taking it and wiping his eyes and then his nose. "Sorry about that," he said at last. "I guess I needed a hug."

"Anytime, Gideon," she said with a soft, compassionate smile. "I...It's weird. I had a dream..."

"Did you? So did I," he answered, as the sheriff made his way over.

"You shouldn't be here, Gideon," the sheriff said, but there was no reprimand in his tone. "But since you are... You wanna come see if you can identify some of the personal items? I'm afraid identifying the body short of dental records isn't going to be possible."

Gideon nodded. "Would you mind waiting a minute, Tracey...Miss Hyun? I'd like to talk to you, but I need to... know," he said to the woman he'd just been flirting with the night before, and on whom he had cried just moments ago. But it wasn't awkward at all. He'd cried on her when Christine had left and when his grandpa Charlie had passed away. The only difference was that this time, he was awake.

"Sure. I'll wait here," she replied. "And Tracey's fine."

He nodded again and followed after the sheriff, under the yellow tape and over to the carefully opened bundle. Mostly bones filled the silt-filled bags, but Christine's Princess-cut diamond engagement ring encircled the left ring finger bones. The beaded wedding gown was tattered and dirty, but it was Christine's gown. And the final proof was the gold chain around the neck and the locket nestled between the clavicles against the sternum now. It had been Christine's mother's locket, and Christine never took it off. Inside should be a photo of Christine as an infant in her mother's arms and the inscription that reads "My Truest Love."

"God," Gideon said in a whisper. Then louder, he said, "Ayuh. This should be Christine Richards. There should be an inscription inside the locket that says, 'My Truest Love.'"

Dom, who was in uniform and kneeling over the remains, reached in with his gloved hand and lifted out the locket. He opened it and confirmed the inscription. "I'm sorry, Gideon," he said softly.

The sheriff nodded and clasped Gideon's shoulder warmly.

"At least now, you know," he said. Gideon nodded.

"Let me know if you need anything," he offered, turning and walking back to Tracey, who smiled sadly and took his arm as they walked away from the lake toward Gideon's truck.

They walked around to the back of the truck. He lowered the tailgate, and they sat side by side. She was dressed in jeans and a tan suede fall jacket that fell to her hips and tied around her waist. Under it, she wore a burgundy cotton turtleneck shirt that clung to her shape like a second skin. If it were any other situation, Gideon would have complimented her appearance, but as it was, it seemed highly inappropriate to do so. Instead, he let out a long, slow breath and pushed his hands at his sides into the tailgate.

She pushed her hair out of her face and spoke first, "I dreamed we watched the Jeoseung Saja reap her soul over the lake. You asked me if he killed her."

"And you told me no; he just led her to the afterlife. Somebody else killed her," he finished.

She blew a breath out of her mouth. "This is weird... right?"

He nodded slowly, staring straight ahead, afraid to

look at her. "It's definitely weird," he answered. That wasn't half of it. Last night was just one of many over a lifetime.

"Is it Christine? Your daughter's mother?" she asked.

"It is," he answered.

"How would I know that? I just met you for real last night. I've never been here in my life. I couldn't know you had a fiancée named Christine and a daughter named Cassie. How could I know that?"

"I have no idea," he answered. "But we have met before. A long time ago."

"Yeah. On a college tour of MIT. You were my student guide." But it was before that, even, he thought.

They were both quiet for a moment. "I told you about Christine…didn't I? In a dream," he finally said.

"Yeah. You've told me everything…in my dreams," she replied. "And I've told you everything." He looked at her. He knew every inch of her body, but he couldn't possibly admit that.

"Your best friend is Gigi Winston…Georgia Glynnis."

"Yours is Scott Unger, your roommate from MIT."

"That Korean shopkeeper in LA freaked you out."

"You thought you saw your grandpa's ghost, but it was just your dad in his underwear."

"That was funny," he laughed.

"Yeah, it was," she laughed as well.

He took her hand into his. "Yeah, this is weird, but I mean…is it really all that different than being online friends or pen pals?"

"It's different…but I get what you mean. We know each other. We're not strangers."

"Exactly," he agreed.

They sat there quietly for a long time. The Medical Examiner arrived. The remains were put into a body bag and removed. The sheriff left. Dom walked over to the two of them. "You two here together?" he asked.

"Hmmmm? What? Oh, no. She's just…consoling me. She happened to come here and see me, is all."

Tracey pointed to her old Impala. "My car's just there," she added. "Deputy Spencer was telling me about his… fiancée. And his daughter."

Dom nodded. "Yeah. He could use someone to talk to right now. Serendipity," he said, smiling, his Jersey accent sounding thick amid all the Maine accents around them.

"Serendipity? I don't think that's the right word…not at all," Gideon said, sadly. "Synchronicity…maybe."

"Yeah. Synchronicity, as defined by Carl Jung…or bittersweet coincidence. But definitely not serendipitous," Tracey agreed.

Dom stared at their interlocked hands and, after a short pause, said, "Okay. Enjoy the synchronicity, I guess." And he walked away. "They're perfect for each other," he grumbled.

Once again, Gideon found himself laughing. The pretty woman next to him laughed, too.

"Have you had that breakfast you were saving your money for yet?" he asked.

"No, not yet," Tracey replied, laying her hand on her stomach.

"There's Bear's Den Restaurant and Tavern in Dover-Foxcroft. Take your car home, and we can go in my truck. I can pick up Cassie at my mom's."

"That sounds nice," she agreed, hopping off the tailgate. "We're connected, Gideon. I don't know how or why, but it's not the worst thing that's ever happened to me...even considering the...um..."

"Dead fiancée?"

"Yeah, that."

"It's not the worst thing that ever happened to me either, though it probably is the worst thing that ever happened to her," he mused. "Bittersweet. I'll follow you."

————

Tracey drove home...funny to call it home; she'd only spent a night in the house, and not a particularly restful one at that. Between the shared dream, in which she experienced all of Gideon's emotions, a fact she had yet to share with him, and the random noises an old house makes, she had very little rest.

She had always considered herself an empath, but this was the strongest connection she had ever shared with anyone in her entire life. She thought she should be scared. It should be a scary thing to share that kind of attachment with emotional closeness and sexual attraction, because that was mingled in the mix, too. The fact that he'd been her dream guy for all those years confused things some. It was hard to tell where the product of her subconscious desires stopped and where the real Gideon started. Oddly enough, it wasn't scary at all but rather comforting...and exhilarating...and exciting...and somehow completely normal feeling. She smiled, thinking about Gideon Spencer. It made her smile. He made her smile. Even if he was experiencing grief.

And she understood intuitively that it wasn't fresh grief. It was grief he'd already processed. He hadn't cried over the loss of Christine so much as regretting his blaming Christine. The love had faded long ago. He was available;

Tracey was certain of that. And he was interested. There was no guilt involved in his asking her out or in the flirting they'd done the night before...or in the way he'd clung to her when he'd realized that the remains were probably those of his runaway bride. They had known each other for nearly a decade.

She took a nervous breath as she pulled into her driveway. The cottage looked almost welcoming in the morning light. With the man following her in his vehicle, she might find the happiness she sought here after all.

She grabbed her purse and threw her keys into it. She excitedly climbed out of her old Impala, a 1969 SS, left to her by her mother, her pride and joy, and the only thing of value she still owned...at least until the lawyer handed over the deed to this farm. She bounded over and climbed up into the passenger side of the big truck. It wasn't new by any means, though much newer than the Impala. Like her own vehicle, it was meticulously clean.

"Hungry?" he asked.

"Starved," she replied.

He smiled and backed out of the driveway. He drove past his tree farm and his trailer and pulled into the driveway of the large farmhouse, a saltbox-style home, where he had grown up.

The house was decorated with bright colored mums in the window boxes and was quite pleasant looking. Gideon had barely pulled into the drive when his mother emerged with 4-year-old Cassie on her hip. She looked like her father, Tracey noted, with blonde hair and blue eyes. His mother stopped short, seeing a girl in the passenger seat, but she recovered quickly from the apparent surprise and opened the back driver's side door, putting the child into her booster.

"Hey, Honey. Did you find anything out?"

"Ayuh. I'll tell you about it later, Mom. Hey, Sweetpea, this is my friend, Tracey. Can you say hello?" he said, looking at the girl in his rearview mirror.

Tracey turned her neck to look at the child with a friendly smile. Cassie blushed and looked at the floor, but obediently squeaked out, "Hello, Miss Tracey."

Gideon's mother smiled and waved over him. "And I'm Nettie Spencer, Gideon's mom," she said, clearly implicating her son's rudeness in not introducing her. Annette Francine Spencer, better known as Nettie, had married Tom Spencer in 1990. Tracey had never met her, but Gideon had told her all about his parents in her dreams.

"It's nice to meet you both," Tracey affirmed with a cordial wave and nod. "I'm Tracey Hyun. Yvette and Paul Ford were my grandparents. I'm living at Goose Fields Farm."

"Hyun? I don't mean to be un-PC, but what kind of name is that? I mean, what nationality? Oh, I sound like a real Karen!" Nettie sputtered.

Tracey laughed kindly. "I know what you're trying to say. Don't feel bad. It's Korean. My father, who died when I was just a baby, was from Seoul, South Korea. Hyun means 'dark' or 'mysterious.' His name was Hyun Seong Min."

"How come your last name is his first name?" asked the child from the backseat.

"Because in Korea, the surname or family name comes first," Tracey answered.

"That's funny," Cassie giggled.

"Yeah, it is, right?" Tracey giggled back.

"So, if Daddy was Korean, his name would be Spencer

Gideon James?" Cassie laughed. "Would I be Spencer Cassandra Dean?" She roared with laughter.

"Uh-huh. But my Korean name isn't Tracey. It's Hyun Soo Shin," she told her.

"Shin, like your leg?" giggled the child.

"Exactly. I like Tracey," she said with a grin.

Nettie hooked Cassie's seatbelt and closed the door. She leaned in Gideon's open window. "Oh, I like her, Gideon."

"Ayuh, I do, too," he answered, rolling up his window and backing out as she stepped back.

Tracey smiled coyly. She had passed the initial test. Daughter. Check. Mom. Check.

Gideon drove into the town of Dover-Foxcroft. There was a moment of awkward silence at first, but he cleared his throat and smiled. "So, Tracey. Sheep farming? Has that been a lifelong dream?" he joked.

She laughed. "Yeah, no. I don't know anything about sheep, and I really have no interest in learning. The lawyer told me there's a farmer who's been taking care of the sheep farm who wants to buy them and the grazing rights on my land. I checked with the head of the agriculture department at my alma mater, and he indicated that the offering price seems fair. I plan on accepting that."

"That farmer would be my brother, Isaac. Your alma mater? That's right, you're a Hokie," he said, smiling.

"I am. I majored in Computer Science. I've been a network administrator at a marketing firm in Richmond for 4 of the last 5 years. I was laid off in January. I've been job hunting since then. It's been a challenging year."

"Right, I knew that," he offered. He was silent for a moment. "Network administrator? That's IT, right?"

She nodded. "It is."

"I think Martin Combs Construction is looking for an IT guy," he offered. "Their office is in town. I can get you their number if you're interested."

"That would be great!" she said, shifting in her seat. A lead on a job. Her decision to come out here to the "wilds of Maine" was looking to be a good one.

"So, you have your BS in Life Sciences and Science, Technology, and Society double major from MIT and an MS and Ph.D. in Biomedical Forensics from Boston University, right?" she asked.

"Ayuh, that's right," he confirmed.

She stared at him. "Um, okay. How…?"

"How did I end up a deputy in Piscataquis County, Maine? I grew up here. I came home. Christine and I were supposed to get married the day after she…I had a job with a lab in Boston, but we were going to have the wedding here, in my church…I just never went back…The truth was neither of us was happy toward the end. That's why I believed… everybody believed…she had just left. Anyway, I like it here," he smiled at her. She knew it all, except for the name of the county. He'd never told her that. The dream guy and the real Gideon really were one and the same. Were *all* the dreams… shared? *All of them?*

"I think I do, too." Tracey agreed.

He pulled into the restaurant's parking lot. The three of them climbed out of the truck and went into the crowded diner. They found a table and ate pleasantly, enjoying each other's company. When the check came, Tracey reached for her wallet. Gideon held up his hand. "Let me get it, Tracey. You can get it next time…after you meet with Mr. Hancock and have more disposable income," he offered.

She sighed in relief. She really needed to be frugal until she had more cash...he was right about that. "Thanks, Gideon. I appreciate it. I'll definitely treat you both once I get some more cash," she said, smiling.

"I need the potty," Cassie announced.

"Oh, alright. Come on," Gideon said to his child, reaching out for her hand.

Cassie shook her head. "I want to go to the *ladies' room*, Daddy," she said with emphasis.

Tracey took the hint. "Oh, sure. I'll take you, Cassie." Cassie took her hand and led Tracey to the restroom. Tracey laughed as the child pulled her along.

When they returned to the table, Gideon was sitting with another man, older than him, also a bit...rougher around the edges...heavier through the middle, less meticulously dressed and groomed, but with similar features. Gideon stood when she and Cassie approached. He sat back down when they were seated.

"Hi, Uncle Isaac," Cassie said, settling into her seat.

"Tracey, this is my brother, Isaac Spencer. Isaac, this is Tracey Hyun," Gideon introduced them.

"You don't look like the bartender from The Love Boat," she giggled.

Gideon was taking a sip of his coffee and choked on it.

Isaac scowled at Gideon. "Now why'd you go and tell her that?" he accused. Then he stuck his hand out hopefully. "I was hoping to meet you, Ms. Hyun. I'd like to make an offer on them sheep."

She shook his hand heartily. "Oh, sure. I absolutely plan on accepting that offer, Mr. Spencer. I have a meeting with Mr. Hancock this afternoon. We can talk after that," she said, smiling.

"You mean it? You're not going to take another offer?" he asked.

Tracey looked at Gideon and sighed contentedly. "You're Gideon's brother. Even if I got a better offer, I'd take yours. It's found money to me," she said. Gideon smiled at her. She locked onto his gaze and smiled back.

Isaac looked back and forth between the two of them. "Oh, crap. I'm sorry. I just walked into a date. I didn't realize. I'll see ye at home, Gid," he stammered, standing and looking around awkwardly. "Um...Cassie, do you wanna come with me and play with Sam and Vivi?"

"Can I?" she asked her father.

"Ayuh, if you like," Gideon replied.

Cassie happily exited with her burly uncle.

Sam was 4 and Vivi was 2. Their mother was Janey Townsend, now Spencer. She and Isaac had been married for 7 years now. Tracey was certain of it.

"My nephew and niece," he volunteered. "Sam is Cassie's age. Vivi is two." He leaned forward. "I have off today. What would you like to do?"

"Can you show me around, Gideon?" she asked with a coquettish smile.

"As I said last night, I'm at your service."

CHAPTER 4

Tracey and Gideon spent all morning together. He showed her all over town. Just before noon, she asked to see where he worked. He blushed. "Really?" he asked. She slipped her hand into his as they walked in the downtown area. They returned to his truck and drove to the Sheriff's office, which was in a red brick building behind the courthouse and attached to the county jail.

They entered the office. A female deputy looked up from her desk as they came through the door. Her face brightened upon seeing Gideon and fell again seeing his hand in Tracey's.

"Hey, Brenda. This is Tracey. Tracey, Brenda Smith. She's dispatch." Gideon introduced them.

"Hi," Brenda said coldly. Then, warmer, to Gideon, she said, "I'm so sorry about Christine, Gideon."

The sheriff emerged from his office and saw the two of them, hand in hand, and cocked his head, quizzically. He approached. "Just the man I was going to come look for," he said, sounding just a little too bright and cheerful.

Gideon's eyes flashed, and Tracey saw hurt in them before he recovered. He sighed heavily. "You aren't serious? You're just eliminating suspects? Right?" he said.

The sheriff frowned.

Gideon huffed and shook his head. "Really? Are you kidding me?"

"Come on back and talk to me, Gideon. Brenda will

take Miss Hyun home."

Tracey suddenly understood. "No. Not a word, Gideon. Not without a lawyer." He squeezed her hand.

"I want an attorney present," he said.

The sheriff nodded and motioned for him to head back to the interrogation room.

Brenda looked crestfallen, but she gathered herself and said to Tracey, "Where do you live?"

"Goose Fields Farm," Tracey answered.

Brenda drove Tracey home in silence. Neither woman spoke to the other. As she pulled into the driveway in front of Goose Fields Cottage, Brenda asked, "Are you dating Gideon?"

"I hope to. I like him," Tracey answered honestly.

"Ayuh, he's a good guy. Smart, ye know," Brenda said.

"Yeah. I know. He is smart. He went to MIT and Boston College. He has a Ph.D., and he uses words like 'synchronicity' correctly," Tracey agreed.

Brenda looked at Tracey and nodded. "Oh. Ayuh, I see it. You talk just like him, only…Southern."

Tracey smiled. "I'm not trying to steal your thunder, Brenda. I don't think he was ever really interested. You know?"

"Ayuh, I know. I still hoped," Brenda said sadly. With that, Tracey exited the vehicle and waved goodbye to Brenda Smith.

Tracey checked her phone. It was a little after noon. Her appointment with Mr. Hancock wasn't until 3. She had nothing to eat in the cottage. She had about $160.00 left. That would be enough for some groceries. She'd seen a Shaw's out on Main in town. She got into her Impala and headed back to town.

She worried about Gideon the entire time she walked around Shaw's, picking out the bare minimum: eggs, milk, bread, butter, ground beef, spaghetti, sauce, baloney, mustard. She checked out and headed back to Goose Fields. She still had over 2 hours to kill. And she was extremely anxious.

She put away her sparse groceries. She paced. She made a baloney sandwich. She ate it without even tasting it. She paced some more.

At 2, her best friend Gigi called.

"Hey, Sweetie," came Gigi's comforting and familiar voice over the phone. "How is it?"

"The farm? It's nice. The house…feels like home," she answered, biting her thumbnail.

"Then why do you sound so stressed? You know you can always just sell it and come home," Gigi offered.

"Oh, I haven't even talked to the lawyer yet, Geege. And I'm going to give this place a chance. I like that I have roots here…even if I didn't know anything about them."

Gigi laughed. "Well, I have to get back to work. My break is over. Don't forget about me," she reminded Tracey for the millionth time.

"I promise I won't forget about you," Tracey chuckled. "Don't forget about me."

Tracey disconnected. She smiled, thinking about her best friend. Gigi was the one true constant in her life. They had been best friends since they were both just 11 years old. In fact, they had exchanged friendship bracelets. They had worked so hard making them. Unfortunately, Tracey had fallen ill and was hospitalized, and the bracelet Gigi had made for her had been lost at MCV. Tracey had been so upset. Gigi had simply hugged her and made her a new one. She looked down at her wrist and straightened the bracelet fondly. Its colors were faded, but she never took it off.

At quarter to three, she headed back into town to the law office of Francis Hancock, Esq.

He was a portly man in his fifties. He gave her the deed to the farm. He handed her a cashier's check for $789,354. "Holy crap!" she exclaimed.

He smiled. "That's just your grandparents' checking and savings accounts. Here is your portfolio. You're a wealthy young lady," he advised her. In addition to the farm, she discovered she owned a few businesses in town, including a florist and a bakery downtown. She also owned part of the construction company Gideon had mentioned to her. Additionally, she owned several houses and an apartment building. "Who manages all of these properties?" she asked.

"Martin Combs," he answered.

"The contractor?"

"Ayuh. You know him?"

"No. Gideon Spencer mentioned him to me. If I wanted to set up an IT consulting firm...how might I go about that?" she asked.

"I'd be happy to help. I have a $2000 retainer fee," he said, smiling.

"You're hired," Tracey laughed, handing him her credit card.

After her meeting with the lawyer, she headed over to the bank to open accounts. She put the vast majority into savings, but opened a checking account with $10,000 and kept $5000 in cash to buy some more groceries and things she needed for the house.

She returned home again. She paced some more. As she was about to make spaghetti, just before 6, there was a knock on her door. She opened it to a harried-looking Gideon.

She threw herself into his arms. He kissed her. Desperation and longing...just the overwhelming need to be with someone...filled them both. She pulled him inside and led him to her bedroom. It had been inevitable. He was going to end up there from the moment she'd grabbed his elbow that morning. And it wasn't like it was the first time. In dreams, it happened often.

He stared at the bed as they crossed the threshold. He grabbed her arm, and she turned to face him. He leaned in and kissed her softly.

"Tracey," he whispered against her mouth. She let out a long sigh, letting her hands trace down his chest to his waist. His breath caught in his chest, and he closed his eyes. She stepped closer. "Are you sure?"

She was breathless and weak in the knees. Unable to form the word, she nodded. He swooped her up in his arms and carried her to the bed, gently laying her on it.

George read through the incident reports. The discovery of a body at Sebec Lake in Piscataquis County practically jumped out at him.

"Lieutenant," he said, pointing out the report. "Are we going to be involved in this investigation?"

"I don't see why we would, Sergeant. The Piscataquis County Sheriff's Department has it under control," his lieutenant replied.

"There's something about it," George pondered. "Mind if I keep an eye on it? I mean, not as an investigator, but just in case…"

"Sure, if you want," his superior officer agreed with a wink.

George nodded. He didn't know what it was about the case that called to him. But it was practically singing his name. He was very interested in the outcome of the investigation. He saw that the fiancé had been questioned. It seemed like a non-starter to him. The young man had an alibi…a good one, and, from the interviews four years ago, he seemed genuinely distraught. He was a deputy, had passed all the psych exams, and had an outstanding record. Of course, officers could be capable of murder and domestic violence. He'd seen it many times over his 32 years in law enforcement…maybe not murder, but certainly the capacity to commit it…and absolutely domestic violence, but nothing about this kid fit into that mold. George's gut said it wasn't the fiancé.

He rocked back in his chair and chewed on the end of a pen. He hadn't been to Sebec Lake in decades. It was God's country up there. He wondered briefly how such a thing could have happened in such a beautiful place, but there was no explanation for the evil in men's hearts.

He thought of Shawn again. He'd dreamt of him last night. It was Christmas. And Shawn and Hannah, George's wife, with their mother, were decorating the Christmas tree. Shawn held his daughter up to put the star on the tree. His wife was laughing. Poor woman had stopped laughing after Shawn's death. And then, George had lost track of her and the kid. She didn't want to see him anyway. He'd failed Shawn… and her.

It was one of the reasons he'd left the Portland PD and taken the job with the State Police.

That night, he and Shawn had finally gotten a break on a string of burglaries they'd been investigating.

It had started in Delaware, and the criminals had worked their way up the East Coast. It started with a combination used car dealership, gun shop, and liquor store. The business model sounded like a terrible idea to begin with, but hey, to each their own. The criminals robbed the safe, took a bunch of guns and ammo, a few bottles of Johnny Walker Black, and a 1967 Corvette...cherry red. The next place they hit was a jewelry store outside Philadelphia. It was the safe cracking that connected the crimes. The criminals used the same method of cutting through the back of the safe instead of the door. And then the note was the clincher. They were brazen criminals. They actually left a note with clues to the next robbery at each crime scene. No one could believe the morons actually signed the notes. Joe and Vince. On every note.

Joe and Vince had made their way to Portland. The pair had burgled a pawn shop. The note hinted at an art gallery being the next target. Hannah, George's wife, had an exhibit there, and the partners were desperate to prevent it.

It all went horribly wrong. Joe and Vince had already broken into the gallery by the time George and Shawn had arrived. Vince seemed as surprised as the partners when Joe, who was one crazy son-of-a-bitch, pulled one of the weapons from the first job in the string. Shawn walked right into it. George watched Shawn get hit from the safety offered by a marble sculpture. Shawn choked and drowned in his own blood, as each heartbeat filled his lungs. Joe grimaced. And ran at the officers breaching the door. George had no choice. He emptied his own weapon's chamber and magazine into

Joe's torso until the crazed man fell beside Shawn.

George sighed heavily. God, he hated the days he relived that night. It never boded well for what would come.

Trent Forrest sat across from George. The younger man was wearing a goofy grin.

"What?" George chuckled.

Trent slid something across the desk toward George. He lifted his hand to reveal an ultrasound. "It's a girl," he announced proudly.

George smiled brightly. Well, that was a pleasant surprise. That's not usually how it went.

———

Gideon pulled Tracey closer, gently caressing her bare shoulder and arm as he caught his breath.

"Mmmm," she moaned, nuzzling his neck below his ear.

"Oh, God," he whispered. "If you keep doing that, I'm never going to go get Cassie, and my brother will definitely come looking for me." He was having a hard time differentiating his dream from reality.

"Ohhhh," she whined. "Let him." She ran her hand down his chest to his hip and sucked gently on his earlobe. His eyes rolled back as he surrendered again, rolling on top of her as she arched her back and wrapped herself around him. He kissed her deeply, their bodies intertwined, undulating in concert, faster and faster, with their heart rates increasing, their breathing heavy, the pleasure mounting. He felt her climax, and he let go, releasing it all: the anguish over what happened to Christine, the frustration over being questioned, and the longing for this beautiful woman beneath him. Reality was way better than the dream.

Spent, he rolled to his back and closed his eyes. He grabbed her hand and squeezed.

"That lived up to…" she started.

"The dreams?" he asked, sitting up and looking at her.

She gasped and nodded. It was true. They had shared *all* those dreams. While reality was better than the dream, they had made love like this many times.

There was suddenly the sound of sirens, and he vaguely noticed the smell of smoke in the air. Someone pounded on the cottage door. He frowned.

"Something's on fire," he exclaimed, grabbing his clothes and quickly pulling on his pants. Tracey quickly dressed while he ran, shirtless, to answer the door.

"Gid…I…uh…" his brother stammered upon seeing him half dressed with his hair mussed, barefoot in the neighbor's house. Isaac shook his head and recovered from his surprise.

"Your trailer is on fire, man. It's like fully engulfed."

"What?" Gideon yelled, pulling his shirt on and starting to step out.

Isaac stopped him, with his arm to his brother's chest. "Shoes, dude. Mom will know…"

Gideon looked down at his bare feet. "Where are my shoes?" he called.

Tracey emerged from the bedroom with his shoes and socks. He pulled on his socks and shoved his feet into the shoes. "Sphinx?" he asked.

"He's out. I saw him in the barn when I noticed the flames," Isaac answered.

Gideon quickly kissed Tracey and ran to his truck. Isaac nodded, waved at her, and followed his younger brother.

The fire department had already arrived, hence the sirens he'd heard earlier. He jumped out of his truck without cutting the engine or shutting the door. The trailer was fully engulfed in flames. He threw up his hands in exasperation.

The sheriff was suddenly standing beside him. "Where have you been?" he asked coolly.

Gideon huffed. "At Goose Fields Cottage. Do you mind?"

"Having dinner?" the sheriff asked.

"None of your business," Gideon answered. "Do I need my lawyer again?"

"Look, Deputy. I'm sorry. I had to ask those questions. Christine was stabbed to death. Repeatedly. Forty-seven times. That indicates a crime of passion, and you are the most likely suspect."

"I would never hurt Christine. Ever," he responded coldly.

"Ayuh, I've confirmed your alibi for the day she went missing. Also, the knife...it was in the bundle. It was a military issue. You never served in the military. I can't completely clear you, but I don't have enough to consider you a viable suspect, either. You can continue to work...but you cannot go near the investigation. You understand?"

"Sheriff. I have the clothes on my back and my truck. Everything else...my weapon, my uniforms, everything, is in my burning home. I'm going to need some time off."

The sheriff nodded. "Ayuh, that you will. Take all the time ye need." He smiled and slapped Gideon on the shoulder.

Sphinx pranced over and wound his way around Gideon's legs. He reached down and scooped the cat up, kissing his head and scratching his jowls. "Hey, Buddy. I'm glad you're safe."

The firefighters slowly extinguished the fire. The trailer was a total loss. The day darkened into night, and Gideon made his way with Sphinx to his parents' house. Cassie was crying. She'd lost everything, too, he reminded himself. He took her from his mother's arms and held her as she cried on his shoulder.

"Where were you?" his mother asked angrily.

"I was…I…Goose Fields Cottage," he stammered, not knowing what to say.

His mother nodded. "Well, at least you were safe. You worried me half to death, Gideon," she scolded.

"I'm sorry, Mom. Really. It's new. And I didn't think. I just wanted to spend time with Tracey. I should have at least told you where I was," he replied.

"Ayuh, you should have! But…I like Tracey. You're an adult, Gideon. You don't have to tell me where you are every second of the day. Cassie can stay here until you work out a place to live. She has some clothes and toys here already. But other than the sofa…we gave Cassie your old room," his mother offered.

"That's okay. He can stay at Goose Fields Cottage," came Tracey's voice behind him. He turned to see her walking up the driveway. "I'm so sorry, Gideon. It looks like…there's nothing left."

CHAPTER 5

A month passed quickly. Gideon and Sphinx came to stay at Goose Fields Cottage. Cassie, at first, stayed with her grandparents, but after a week, she started staying in one of Tracey's upstairs bedrooms, the one that had been her mother's childhood room.

There were two rooms on the second floor. Tracey set about setting up one as a home base for her new business. The other, her mother's room, she happily allowed the child to have. She found she enjoyed having the girl around. She certainly enjoyed having Gideon around. By Halloween, she told him she didn't want either of them to leave.

"Are you saying you want to live together, Tracey?" he asked, leaning against the kitchen counter. He put his hands on her hips and pulled her against him.

She put both hands on his chest, looked him right in the eye, and responded, "I'm saying we already live together, and I would like for us to continue doing so."

"Ayuh. Me too," he said, flashing that rakish, charming smile of his. Then, more seriously, he added, "So, what do we do? Do I pay you rent? How do we split living expenses?"

"Oh," she said, drawing back. "I really hadn't thought about that. You're right, though. We should have that sort of thing clearly defined." She thought for a moment. "I don't have a mortgage, so I don't feel right demanding rent. I need the Wi-Fi for my business, so I should pay for that. But maybe you could pay the utilities...and we can split the groceries and cable?" she suggested.

"That seems fair," he agreed. "You want to get Mr. Hancock to draw up a formal agreement?"

She laughed and kissed him. "MIT. I forgot. Of course, you're pragmatic."

"Ayuh, it may not be very romantic, but we'll both feel better with our responsibilities clearly outlined. If we get married, we can…renegotiate."

"When," she mumbled as she walked away.

"I heard that," he teased.

"Good," she called over her shoulder.

Rural trick or treating was a new experience. It required a vehicle. In the barn, she had discovered an ATV. This was the vehicle that was used. Gideon and Cassie took the ATV out at 4 pm, while Tracey stayed home. She was surprised by the number of trick-or-treaters. She didn't expect many, given her location so far out of town, but the kids from the surrounding farms all showed up…some on ATVs like Cassie and Gideon, some in 4-wheel-drive trucks, but all with a parent, who waited in the vehicle while the kids ran to her door and rang her bell. She was glad she had listened to Gideon and bought treats.

It was interesting that they all seemed to know who she was and that she was with Gideon. She was insta-accepted as his girlfriend.

Just as the trick-or-treating seemed to slow, there was a knock at the door. Tracey opened the door expecting more cute, costumed kids, but found a middle-aged couple instead. The woman had stunning silver hair. The man was a little overweight, balding, but robust. His hands were rough. He was used to working, she noted.

"Oh, hello," the woman said, peering into the door. "I'm sorry. We vere told Gideon Spencer and Cassie vere living here." She seemed almost nervous. Her accent was Eastern European.

"They do. They're trick-or-treating. Um…they should be back soon. Would you like to come in?" Tracey offered.

"Vould you…mind?" the woman asked.

"Of course not. Please," Tracey offered. The couple came through the door. "Would you like some coffee or tea, or something?"

"Coffee vould be nice, thank you," the woman replied, sitting on the sofa in front of the cottage's massive stone, colonial fireplace, in which a cozy fire burned. Tracey excused herself and went to the kitchen to prepare the coffee, returning a few minutes later with three cups, cream and sugar, and spoons on a serving tray.

"Are you Gideon's girlfriend?" the woman asked, taking a cup of coffee.

"Isn't that obvious, Lena?" the man chuckled. "Sorry. I'm Gary Richards. This is my wife, Lena. We're…um… Christine was our daughter," he said.

"Oh. You're Cassie's grandparents. Oh. Nice to meet you. Yes, I'm Tracey Hyun, and yes, I am Gideon's girlfriend." She blushed, saying it out loud, but it made her happy to say it.

Gideon and Cassie burst through the front door. Cassie was dressed as a cute little witch. She pointed her "magic wand" at her father. "Abbacadabba! You's a frog, Daddy!" she said.

"Ribbit, ribbitt," he said, jumping. Cassie laughed hysterically.

"Abbacadabba. You's a puppy," she giggled.

"Woof, woof," Gideon said, scooping her up into his arms. Then he saw the Richards. "Hi," he said. He set Cassie back down. "Um, Cassie. This is your Grandma and Grandpa Richards...your mommy's parents."

The Richards stayed for an hour or so. They had gifts for Cassie, among them a porcelain doll. She had long, braided dark brown hair and rosy cheeks. She was dressed in a multicolored costume with a white blouse with long sleeves, red ribbons tied at the elbows, a red vest, and a multicolored horizontal striped skirt.

"How pretty," Tracey noted as Cassie held up the doll.

"She is dressed in the national costume of Serbia, vere I vas born," Lena explained, her Eastern European accent heavy.

"You're Serbian? How interesting. I'm learning about my Korean heritage now. I think it's important to have a sense of our heritage," Tracey said, conversationally.

"I couldn't agree more," Lena confirmed.

They were very cordial. And Cassie had fun.

As they left, Lena Richards thanked Tracey for her hospitality. "We left Boston shortly after Christine disappeared," she explained. "I couldn't bring myself to see Cassie...or Gideon. He asked us to come see her. Well, we vere in Boston this week. I thought we should try...Thank you for letting us see her."

"I have nothing to do with that, Mrs. Richards. That's completely up to Gideon."

After Gideon got Cassie to bed, he sat quietly watching the fire in the fireplace while Tracey took a bath.

She found him staring at the dying embers with Sphinx

on his lap when she emerged, rosy and scrubbed from the bathroom after a long soak. "Should I not have invited them in?" she asked, sitting beside him.

"Hmmm? Oh, no. It's fine. They're good people. I've wanted them to meet Cassie for a long time. I'm glad they finally made the effort."

"So, what's wrong then?" she asked.

He sighed. "I don't know. Nothing you did. I'm just... uneasy. I don't know why." He smiled at her and put his arm around her. "Don't let it scare you off, Baby. It's just a mood."

She smiled and lay up against him. "I'm not easily scared," she replied.

Later, Tracey fell asleep in Gideon's arms.

The night seemed particularly dark as a storm front moved in during the middle of the night. The rain started around 3 am. And so did the dream. The Jeoseung Saja hovered over Sebec Lake. "What do you want?" Tracey called to the monster from the shore.

"I am not your enemy," the creature replied, its voice raspy and ancient. "Do not fear me."

"You don't exactly look friendly," she called back, as Gideon took her hand, pushing her behind him to stand between her and the Reaper.

"Your fear dictates my appearance. But I will never harm you, Hyun Soo Shin. Nor you, Gideon Spencer. I'll not say your names again. Look to the boathouse. Becky Hawk lies within. Becky Hawk's time is done. Becky Hawk joins me now."

Then the Reaper's appearance changed. The darkness lifted some, as the sky lit up with lightning, and his face was visible for a brief moment. It was a young Korean male face, handsome. His pallor warmed, and for a brief second, he appeared as a living man. Then the lightning ceased as thunder rolled, and the shadow enveloped the Reaper's form again. Becky Hawk's spirit emerged from the boathouse. The Reaper opened his arms, and the ghost entered the swirling shadows around him. Tracey pushed past Gideon and called out to the Reaper, "Appa! Don't go! Daddy, come back! Appa!"

"Daddy?" Gideon asked, pulling her close as the Jeoseung Saja disappeared.

Tracey sat bolt upright in the bed. Gideon stirred and took her hand. "Tracey," he said softly, as she started to cry. "Appa…means 'father'?"

She nodded. "That thing was my father," she sniffed. He sat up beside her.

"Becky Hawk is in the boat house," he said.

"So says my dad," she agreed. "Who's Becky Hawk?"

"One of the three women who vanished on Greeleys Landing Road this year. The third, in fact. She went missing after the 4th of July weekend…on July 8th, Tuesday night. We had a big storm. Her car was found at Greeleys Landing on the 9th."

"We had the same dream again, huh?" she said, just to clarify.

"Ayuh," he replied, holding her close. She wrapped her arms around him and held on for dear life.

"Why did he say he wouldn't say our names again?" Gideon asked.

"If a Jeoseung Saja says your name three times, you die," Tracey answered.

"Oh. Great," Gideon smirked. "Hey, Appa. Really…

keep my name out of your mouth!" he joked.

"Stop, Gideon," Tracey implored, hugging him tighter.

———

Morning came, as it always does. The storm had moved on as well, but it left the day gray, wet, and chilly. Tracey and Gideon spent the rest of the weekend working on the house. It was generally in good condition, having been recently remodeled, but having spent a month living in it, Tracey had discovered a few drafty spots. Gideon helped shore up the windows and doors that contributed to the drafts. And Cassie wanted her room to be pink, so they spent the weekend painting it, while Cassie stayed with Gideon's parents. Tracey even bought new curtains and bedding for the little girl, to make the space her own, since they had decided to make the living situation permanent.

Monday morning came quickly. Gideon was scheduled to return to work. Despite not yet having received his insurance payout, he had replaced his uniform, lost in the fire, and dressed quickly in it to combat the chill of the house. He started a fire in the fireplace before he left the cottage, driving the cruiser into Dover-Foxcroft to report for duty. He drove to Dunkin first and picked up 4 coffees and a dozen donuts.

He arrived at the office just before 7. He parked his cruiser, a 4-wheel-drive SUV, and carried in the coffee and donuts. Inside, he smiled brightly, offering Brenda a coffee. "Good morning," he said cheerily. "It's good to be back at work."

"It's good to have you back," Brenda replied, taking a coffee. "Still living with the new girlfriend?"

"Ayuh. In fact, we've decided to make it permanent. I can officially put in my change of address," he answered with a wink.

"Great," grumbled Dom, accepting a coffee as well. "Not like you aren't chipper enough in the morning."

Gideon laughed. "Why does my good mood make your bad mood worse?" he asked.

"I dunno," Dom said. "It just does." Then he smiled.

The sheriff emerged from his office. "Welcome back, Deputy," he said. "Did I hear you're officially changing your address to Goose Fields Farm?"

"Ayuh. The cat, the kid, and I are all very happy about it…and Tracey is…just the best," he answered with a lovesick smile.

The sheriff laughed heartily. "I haven't seen that goofy look on your face in years. Congratulations, Gideon. Really. I'm happy for you."

"Thanks, Ralph. That means a lot," he replied. Weird ass dream or not, today he was in a great mood, and nothing was going to interfere with that.

He went out on a few calls in the morning. Mrs. Stewart's cat was stuck in a tree. Shaw's caught a couple of teenage girls shoplifting in the cosmetics section. Tim Patterson rear-ended Harry Morgan at Goff's Corner when he thought Harry had pulled through the intersection, but he hadn't. Tim had been on a conference call with his broker in Portland and was distracted.

At lunch, Tracey and Cassie met him at Bear Den Restaurant and Tavern. She had asked Mr. Hancock for a rental agreement outlining the terms they had discussed. It was a simple contract that just required minor alterations, so he had it ready by 11, and she showed up at the restaurant with it. Gideon happily signed, sealing the deal with a kiss over burgers and fries.

"I have a client meeting this afternoon, so your mom is meeting me here to pick up Cassie," she told him, putting away the contract. "The bank in town needs a system update."

"Oh, okay. Good luck, Babe. That sounds like a great opportunity for you."

She smiled and leaned forward. "I know. I'm really excited about it," she said, shimmying in her seat. "It's my first big client. Other than your brother, I haven't had much work yet." Isaac, after he had purchased her livestock and grazing rights on her land, had asked her to set up a network for his farm. It had only taken a week to install, and she'd offered a good rate given she was sleeping with his brother. Anything else would have felt like taking advantage of family.

"I want to head to the bank, too," Gideon advised, taking a bite of his burger. "I want to put you on my safe deposit box and make you the beneficiary of my assets."

"What assets?" she teased.

"I have assets," he said, grinning.

As they finished eating, Nettie Spencer came in, smiling and waving with both hands.

"Granny!" Cassie squealed, jumping up and running to her grandmother. "Guess what? Daddy and me are going to stay living at Tracey's house! Idn't that cool?"

"Ayuh, very cool," Nettie replied, laughing. "So, you're official, now?" she asked, scooping up her granddaughter and turning to her son and his new girlfriend.

"We're official, now," he laughed.

His radio went off. "Charlie 4-9, respond. 10-54 at Greeleys Landing boat house. Advise of ETA."

Tracey went pale. He patted her hand and responded.

"Dispatch, Charlie 4-9 responding. Understand 10-54 at Greeleys Landing boat house. ETA 10 minutes."

"10-54. Is that what I think it is?" Tracey asked.

He nodded. "I have to go to work, Babe. Good luck at the bank. Cassie, be good for Granny."

CHAPTER 6

Gideon pulled his cruiser up to the boathouse entrance and climbed out from behind the wheel. Jim Perkins, the boathouse and dock manager, stepped forward. He was nearly 60 now and had held this job for more than 35 years. "Oh, dear God," he exclaimed, shaking uncontrollably and near tears. "I ain't never seen nuthin' like this." He wrung his hands as he spoke.

"It's alright, Mr. Perkins. Show me," Gideon said calmly, laying a comforting hand on the old man's arm. Jim nodded and pointed along the side of the boathouse.

"She was floatin' face down, bumpin' up against the dock there. I...I thought it was a sack. So, I went to fish it out of the water, and it turned over. Oh God, I nearly died of fright," Jim explained excitedly. "It...she...looks like that nice Miss Hawk...from the bank. But there ain't no way she's been dead for 4 months, Gideon. I mean, she looks bad...but she's still recognizable."

Gideon walked down the dock to where the body was still floating. He snapped on gloves. "Oh, God," he said, pulling her onto the shore. He did a cursory examination of the body. She had abrasions on her hands, feet, and knees. There was bruising around her neck. Her hands were bound behind her back. The rope was tied in a constrictor knot. And Jim was right. No way she died 4 months ago. She'd been in the water maybe 3 or 4 days, tops. Further, she wasn't wearing the clothes she had been wearing when she disappeared in July. The dress she had on was a purple woolen sweater dress...

currently in season…put on sale at the boutique in town last month. His mother had bought one in a robin's egg blue. He took out his camera and started documenting everything.

Seconds later, the sheriff was beside him. "What do you think, Gideon?" he asked.

"I think she was alive until 3 or 4 days ago. I think she was held in a cabin around here somewhere. Which means, the other two missing women…might still be alive, too," Gideon said.

"Ayuh, I think yer right. We'll set up a canvas of all the cabins around here. Meanwhile, check at that boutique to see if anyone remembers someone buying this dress. And go talk to Howard Charleston at the bank. See if anything stands out about the last few days before Miss Hawk disappeared. Take Dom with you."

Gideon nodded and pulled off his gloves. He walked away, stooping under the crime scene tape a young state forest ranger was putting up. He climbed back into his cruiser and sat there for a moment. He sighed and started the engine, driving back into town.

He pulled up outside the Sheriff's Office. Dom was waiting for him at the door. He walked over and got into the passenger side. Gideon pulled away and drove toward the bank.

———

Tracey shook Mr. Charleston's hand. She smiled warmly as she took a seat across from him at his desk. "Good afternoon," she started. "I have a cursory idea of what you want with your system update. I'm new to the area, but I'm here to stay. My grandparents left me their property, and I've formed strong relationships here. I'd love to work with you,

Mr. Charleston."

"Ayuh, I hear through the grapevine you and the Spencer boy are livin' together. He's well-liked around these parts. And your grandparents were good people. I went to school with your mother, myself. Of course, I was a few years ahead of her," he said, smiling coyly.

Smiling like a wolf in sheep's clothing, Tracey thought, but she nodded enthusiastically. A *few* years indeed. More like 5 or 6, she mused.

"Well, I've reviewed your proposal, and I think we can work together well enough. We'd like to get started as soon as possible. Can you start this week?"

"Absolutely. I can start tomorrow morning, if you like," Tracey answered.

"Great. We'll see you tomorrow then, Miss Hyun." Mr. Charleston stood, signaling her time was up. She smiled again and stood, shaking his hand once more. She exited his office to see Gideon, her Gideon, and Dom Moretti enter the bank. Gideon winked at her as she gave a quick wave and walked past him and out the door.

She glanced at the time on her phone and decided she had time to run to Shaw's. They had groceries, but she wanted to celebrate. Steak and lobster…and a good bottle of wine…maybe some flowers from the florist she owned for the table. She drove to Shaw's, and walking on air, she entered the store.

She asked for help at the live lobster tank. "Fresh from Portland, this morning," the fishmonger assured her. She bought two. She got some fresh asparagus, a couple of potatoes, some clarified butter, a bottle of Cabernet Sauvignon, and two huge ribeye steaks.

"You and Gideon celebrating something special tonight?" asked the woman behind her in the checkout line. She was about her age, slightly overweight, generally nondescript, not someone who particularly stood out or drew notice. Tracey could swear she had never seen the woman before, let alone met her.

"Um…yeah," she answered, surprised by the woman's knowledge of her affairs.

The woman laughed. "It's a small town, Honey. We all know everything."

"Really?" Tracey asked, laughing.

"Sure. For example, he fell hard the night you showed up, and you stopped at the Stop Buy convenience store because of the rain. He stayed there talking to you for over an hour. And the next day, he took you all over town, even though that was the day they found poor Christine's remains."

"That's all true," Tracey confirmed.

"He moved in with you that night," the woman whispered, leaning closer.

"That's true, too, but his house did burn down… And I fell for him hard, too."

The woman laughed again, good-naturedly. "Who wouldn't?"

"Exactly," Tracey laughed back, but the woman made her very uncomfortable.

The checkout clerk bagged her items. She swiped her newly acquired debit card.

"Have fun," the strange woman said.

"We will," Tracey replied.

She stopped at the florist and picked a beautiful fall arrangement for the table. Then she got back into her old

Impala and started home. Gretchen Banks waved to her as she drove past the Stop Buy. Neither woman saw the black SUV following her.

————

Dom asked to be taken back to the Sheriff's office as he and Gideon left the bank. He had a dentist's appointment, he said. He claimed his mood that morning had been due to a toothache, and he'd just gotten a text message that the dentist could squeeze him in. Gideon happily complied. Anything to improve Dom's mood.

He then headed back out to the boutique. It was a small, locally owned shop in a strip mall out by Shaw's. Mrs. Kerry, his first-grade teacher, now retired, worked there part-time. He strode into the small shop and waved to Mrs. Kerry, who was helping a customer.

Once she was free, she greeted him warmly, "Hello, Gideon! My, aren't you handsome in your uniform? Are you looking for a gift for your pretty, new girlfriend? We just got in these beautiful Dongsimgyeol knot bracelets. They're a Korean love knot. And we have lots of gorgeous colors," she said, making a game show hostess hand sweep to showcase the aforementioned bracelets.

"Oh, no. I'm here on official business. I have questions about somebody who may have bought three of those woolen sweater dresses like my mom bought last month. Ohhhh. The burgundy one, please. That will match that shirt I like," he said, pointing to one of the bracelets.

Mrs. Kerry grinned as she took the silken thread rope bracelet from the case and draped it across the palm of her hand. "Oh, this will look lovely against her complexion. Come to think of it, there was someone who bought three of those dresses. The odd thing about it was that not one was in her size, and they were all three different sizes. I supposed she must have been on a diet and bought them as goal items."

"A woman? Do you know who she was?" he asked. "How much?" he nodded at the bracelet, taking out his wallet.

"$14.64," she answered. "No. I'd never seen her before. An out-of-stater camping at the state park, I'd say."

He handed her a twenty. She gave him his change and put the bracelet into a gift box and then into a pretty, little burlap bag with a silk ribbon to tie it shut and the store's logo printed on the burlap.

"What colors and sizes did she buy, Mrs. Kerry?" he asked, taking the purchase from her.

"Oh, let me think. It was a navy in a size 14, an eggplant in a size 10, and an ecru in a size 6."

"You wouldn't happen to know the sizes of some of your customers, would you?"

"I would if I have a card on them."

He smiled. "How about Hailey Burns, Grace Kemp, and Becky Hawk?"

She gasped. "Oh dear! Do you have a lead? Oh, let me see," she replied, grabbing a tin file card box from under the counter. "Hailey Burns…size 14. I don't have a card for Grace Kemp. Um…Becky Hawk, size 10."

"Eggplant…that's purple?"

"Yes."

Becky had been wearing a purple dress.

"How many of the purple in size 10 did you sell?" he asked.

"Oh, we only had one in the purple…it was our only size 10," Mrs. Kerry answered.

Gideon was flummoxed. At the bank, he learned that there was a rumor Becky had started seeing someone in the last few months before her disappearance. The gossip around the proverbial water cooler was that *he* might be married, as she was being very cagey about *him*...and now, he had discovered a woman had purchased the dress Becky was found wearing. Still, he hadn't identified either the mystery man or the out-of-stater woman. He knew for a fact there was no boyfriend, but she was indeed seeing someone. Could it be the same woman?

He walked back to his cruiser and saw Tracey's old Impala pull out of Shaw's parking lot. A black SUV followed her. He cocked his head. There was nothing unusual about a black SUV, but he had that uneasy feeling. He decided just to see in which direction the SUV went.

He followed and saw the Impala park at the florist. The SUV pulled into a street parking space. Tracey got out of the Impala and entered the florist. Nobody got out of the SUV. A few minutes later, Tracey came out carrying a flower arrangement. She got back into her car and pulled back into traffic. The SUV followed.

"What the hell?" he muttered, following again at a safe distance to remain undetected.

CHAPTER 7

Tracey, about 3 miles out of town, remembered she also needed milk, as Sphinx had knocked the jug off the counter this morning when she had looked away. She made a U-turn and headed back in the direction of Dover-Foxcroft, planning to stop at the convenience store for the milk. To her surprise, she passed Gideon in his cruiser. To her horror, the SUV behind her also made a U-turn.

She stopped at the store, got the milk, and got back into the Impala. Frighteningly, the black SUV was in the parking lot, even though nobody had come into the store behind her. She pulled back onto Greeleys Landing Road. The SUV followed. She pressed the accelerator, getting up to 70 miles per hour. The SUV sped up, faster and faster, gaining on her quickly.

She floored it. The SUV started to overtake her. The vehicle rammed into her rear bumper. The Impala shimmied on the road. She grasped the wheel and somehow regained control of the vehicle. She braked, reducing her speed. The SUV started to pass her, only it plowed into her instead, pushing her off the road. She hit the soft shoulder of the blacktop, and the Impala flipped and slid on its roof. Her life flashed in front of her eyes, but the seatbelt held, and she hung upside down, staring, completely disoriented, out the spiderwebbed windshield. The milk, groceries, and flowers were scattered throughout the car cab. She had a bump on her forehead, and her neck hurt. She didn't know if she had hit her head on the steering wheel, or window, or if the vase holding the flowers or wine bottle had hit her as it flew through the cab, or if all three things had happened. The milk jug had busted open, and she and the interior of the car were soaked with milk. She screamed uncontrollably with pure terror as someone yanked the driver's side door open and cut her seatbelt, pulling her out of the wrecked vehicle.

"Tracey, Baby, it's me. Honey, stop. It's me," Gideon's voice yelled as she screamed and blindly hit and kicked at the person pulling her from the car.

Slowly, she realized she wasn't about to be gruesomely murdered and collapsed into his arms, crying. "My car!" she wailed. He sat on the ground, pulling her into his lap as he leaned his back against his cruiser.

"Your car?" he sniffed, holding her tightly. "Someone tried to kill you, Trace. Fuck the car."

Tracey realized what had happened. She clung to Gideon, shaking as she cried. "I planned a special dinner. I got lobsters and ribeyes…and wine…and flowers. Oh, my head…my neck…my ccccaaaarrrr," she wailed. He wrapped his arms around her and held her tightly for what seemed only a moment, but apparently was several minutes.

The sheriff pulled up. "Gideon," he said softly, placing his hand on his deputy's shoulder. "I need you to let go, Son. The EMTs need to check her injuries. Let go."

That's when Tracey realized Gideon was crying, too. He released his hold on her and wiped his eyes as he struggled to catch his breath.

"She's his girlfriend," the sheriff explained as the EMTs moved to load her onto a board. "You okay to drive, Gideon?" Gideon nodded as he calmed and pulled himself to stand. He stumbled to get back behind the wheel of his cruiser.

"I'll follow the ambulance," he said quietly.

"Alright. I'll wait for the tow truck, and I'll meet you at the hospital to get your statements," the sheriff said as Tracey was lifted to a gurney and loaded into the back of the ambulance.

———

Gideon followed the ambulance to Northern Light Mayo Hospital in Dover-Foxcroft. He parked and raced into the emergency room waiting area.

"My girlfriend…" he sputtered.

"Ah. I see. Sorry, officer. I can't let you back. Family only. But can you tell us her next of kin?"

"Me. I'm it. She doesn't have any family," he exclaimed.

The nurse calmly responded, "I'm sorry. You can wait out here, but family only."

He paced for the next hour, biting his thumbnail into the quick.

Tracey emerged through the double doors in a wheelchair, pushed by a large orderly. Her arm was in a sling, her neck in a brace. She had a black eye and a fat lip.

"God, Tracey," Gideon exclaimed upon seeing her. He rushed forward, kneeling in front of her.

She smiled weakly. "I'm okay. I have a hairline fracture on my wrist, whiplash, and a few bumps and bruises. No concussion."

"Thank God," he breathed. He laid his head on his arm on the armrest of the wheelchair.

He felt more than saw the man step up behind him. He looked over his shoulder to see the sheriff. "Hey, you two. You okay, Miss Hyun?"

"I'd nod, but I can't," Tracey joked. "Yeah, I'm okay."

"Feel up to telling me what happened?"

"Sure," she said, as Gideon stood up and took the wheelchair from the orderly. He pushed her over to an empty corner. The sheriff followed, taking out his traffic accident report form. Tracey explained how the black SUV had followed her and chased her down, running her off the road.

"Did this SUV hit you?"

"Yes. It rammed me in the rear, and it pushed me off the road."

"So, there would be damage to its front end and passenger side?" the sheriff queried.

"Yeah, there should be," she answered.

"Did you get a plate number or a make and model?"

"No. Sorry."

"Late model GMC Yukon Denali…maybe 2022. Maine plates 452-FMN. Reported stolen off an Olds Intrigue from Bath two days ago," Gideon said, starting to pace again. Realizing both Tracey and the sheriff were looking at him, he added. "What? I saw it following Tracey, and I trailed it. I ran a check on the plates. I got the report back after it ran her off the road. I should have stopped it."

"Had it committed any traffic violations?" the sheriff asked him.

"No."

"Then you had no cause to make a stop," the sheriff said. "Look, Son, hindsight is 20/20. Tracey's okay. We'll catch the guy."

"Or woman," Tracey interjected.

"What do you mean? Did you see the driver?" Gideon asked.

"No. No. I…I just had this really weird interaction with a strange woman at Shaw's. I… I've never seen her before, but she knew everything about us. She told me how, when, and where we met, and how you stayed for over an hour to talk to me…how you spent all morning the next day with me, even though that was the day Christine's remains…how you moved in with me that night…It was kind of creepy."

"Huh…huh…huh," Gideon gasped, putting his hand to his head. "What did she look like?"

"Um…my age, maybe. Dark hair, dark eyes. Olive complexion. Plus-sized."

"Son of a bitch," he exclaimed. He grabbed the sheriff's elbow and pulled him out of earshot. "Mrs. Kerry told me they had one dress in that purple. It was sold to a woman matching that description, along with two other dresses in two different sizes. The purple was Becky's size. Mrs. Kerry didn't have a size for Grace, but one of the other dresses was in Hailey's size," he whispered.

"Fuck," said the sheriff. "Good work. Keep an eye on your girl."

———

Gideon was so worried about Tracey. She smiled as he lifted her out of the wheelchair to sit her in the passenger seat of his police cruiser.

"I can stand and walk, you know?" she teased him.

"I know, but just for tonight, please let me take care of you. Please," he pleaded. She grabbed his hand.

"What's going on?" she asked, smiling.

"How long do you have to wear that neck thing?"

"Ten days. Why?" she asked, curious about what was on his mind. He looked positively miserable.

"So, in 11 days…would you…like to marry me?" He was staring at the ground.

"I'm sorry…what?" Tracey asked. He had mumbled. Had she heard him correctly?

He held his head up and looked her in the eyes. "On Saturday, the 15th…in 11 days, would you…will you marry me?"

She sat there with her mouth open. "I know we've moved really fast, Honey," she started after several seconds of awkward silence. "But don't you think that would be really, really fast?" It wasn't. They both knew it wasn't. It was 10 years, not a month.

"Ayuh. But, they wouldn't let me back to see you or tell me anything. And…I realized that I want to be your person. The person who's there for you in everything. And I want that for the rest of my life. What's more, I want you to be my person. And it doesn't matter that I've only known you a month. In fact, it's great. That means we can be each other's people for longer."

"Oh, Honey. That's some messed-up logic," she giggled.

"I don't care. I still wanna marry you…and you said 'when'," he proclaimed.

"I said 'when'? I don't know what that means," she replied.

"I said, 'If we get married,' and you said, 'When,'" he said. She sighed. "I know it sounds cr…"

"Yes," she said, surprising herself. But by God, she meant it. She wanted it.

"Yes?" He spun around, excitedly. Then he yelled, "She said 'yes'!"

An older couple was getting into their car three parking spaces away. "Congratulations," the man said. The woman clapped.

Gideon laughed and leaned into the cruiser to kiss her. Then he grinned, biting his bottom lip. "You need a ring. Let's go buy a ring."

"Sure. But can we do that tomorrow? I just really want to go home," she answered.

"Ayuh, anything you want, Baby." Then he remembered the bracelet. He reached past her and grabbed the little burlap bag. "This will do for the moment," he said, removing the little box and opening it. He took the bracelet out and tied it to her wrist beside the friendship bracelet she wore.

He drove home with a big grin on his face. She must have been grinning, too. Her cheeks started to hurt.

He stopped at his parents' house to get Cassie. His mother came out with his daughter.

"Hey, you're later than I expected. Oh my God, Tracey, what happened?" Nettie Spencer said.

"Tracey had a car accident," Gideon explained. "Sorry we're late."

"Ayuh, well, that's a good excuse," his mother sputtered.

"Oh, and we're getting married on the 15th," he announced.

"What?" his mother said as she was putting Cassie into the backseat.

————

At Goose Fields Cottage, he carried Tracey inside. Cassie skipped in front of them, opening the door. He put

Tracey on the sofa. "Hungry?" he asked. "I'm afraid I can't do lobster and steak, but I make a mean ham sandwich," he teased.

Tracey laughed. "A ham sandwich is fine," she answered.

"How about you, Cassie? Ham sandwich?"

"Can I have peanut butter and jelly?" his daughter asked.

"Ayuh, I think I can make that," he said, grabbing her up and carrying her under his arm like a book into the kitchen. She laughed.

"Daddy!" she squealed. "You're silly."

Once inside the kitchen, he set her down and kneeled on one knee, holding her shoulders gently and looking her in the eyes. "Cassie, Sweetpea, Tracey and I want to get married. How do you feel about that?"

She cocked her head and pursed her lips. "Mmmmm. I think it's good. Tracey is good. She's a good mommy."

"She's a good Mommy?" he asked, astounded by his daughter, as usual.

"Ayuh, she's already my mommy. She reads me stories and tucks me in at night. She gives me a bath. She helps me get my shoes on the right foot. And she gives me hugs and kisses every day. Isn't that a mommy?"

He felt the lump form in his throat and tears fill his eyes. Damn, he was turning into a crybaby. He nodded. "Ayuh, it sure is."

He watched as Cassie skipped back into the living room. She climbed up onto the sofa beside Tracey.

"Are yous hurt?" she asked sweetly.

"A little," Tracey answered. "But not so bad I can't

read you a book," she offered.

"Yay!" Cassie exclaimed, jumping down and running to retrieve a book. Gideon nearly choked when she returned with *Are You My Mother?* Tracey didn't react at all. She read the book, holding her arms straight out in front of her in what had to be the most uncomfortable position for reading ever.

He made the sandwiches, two ham, one peanut butter and jelly, and added some chips to the plates. He loaded up his arms, waiter style, and carried them into the living room. "I thought we'd have a sofa picnic," he announced. He set the plates on the coffee table. "What can I get you ladies to drink?"

"All we have is Coke. Sphinx knocked the milk over this morning. Speaking of which, I'm getting rank. The milk I bought to replace it busted open in the accident, and I'm kinda wearing it," Tracey noted, holding her arm up to her nose and making a face.

He laughed. "How about we peel those off you, and you wear your robe until after we eat. Then I can help you shower."

"I'll get your robe and slippers, Tracey," Cassie volunteered, running off to retrieve the items. Gideon pulled Tracey to stand and gingerly pulled the offending clothes off as Cassie returned with the robe. She slipped it on and shimmied out of her underwear and bra with the skill of an escape artist under the robe. He blinked hard, shook his head, and took the clothes to the washing machine. He returned with three Cokes.

The three of them ate around the coffee table. He added a log to the fireplace and started a fire. He led Tracey to the master bathroom, helped her shower, and wash her hair. He found a pair of flannel pajamas and clean underwear, helped her dress, and led her back to brush her hair out in front of the fire.

Cassie snuggled up next to Tracey. "Am I getting married, too?" she asked.

"Yes," Tracey answered, giving her shoulders a squeeze. "The three of us are getting married."

Gideon smiled. He was so happy. He leaned down and kissed Tracey's head before brushing all those lovely black curls again.

He got Cassie bathed and put her to bed.

Tracey's phone rang. He retrieved it from her purse and handed it to her. The caller ID read "Gigi." She swiped it and put the call on speaker so she could relax her neck. "Heya, Gigi. How's it goin'?" she greeted the caller.

"Hey! Girl! OMG! I've been so swamped since you left! How are you doin'? Do you like it in Maine?"

"Mmmm. Yeah. It's great. I wrecked my car today, but my boyfriend proposed, so I came out on the plus side."

"Oh, Cal is being a butt...wait, what did you just say?" came the voice on the other end of the call.

"I said I'm getting married!" Tracey squealed. "Ow," she continued in a quieter tone, putting her hand to her neck.

"You're...are you nuts? You've only been gone a month," said her friend.

"Hold on. Gideon, come here. Take a picture of us," she said, handing him the phone. He leaned his face next to hers and snapped a selfie. He handed her back the phone. She sent the photo via text. "Keep in mind, I totaled the Impala and look like I've been in an MMA match."

"You totaled the Impala?"

"Yeah, I flipped it."

"Oh, Honey. I'm so sorry...oh, he's cute," Gigi said. Gideon laughed. "What did you call him? Gideon? Like the Bibles?"

"Ayuh, sort of," he interjected. "Do you know that Beatles song, *Rocky Raccoon*?"

Gigi burst out laughing. "You're named for a line in a Beatles song? That's awesome. Is that a badge?"

"Ayuh, I'm a deputy with the Piscataquis County Sheriff's Department," he told her.

"How old are you?"

"29," he answered dutifully.

"Ever been married?"

"Almost, but no. I do have a 4-year-old daughter named Cassie," he answered.

"Religion?"

"Baptized Lutheran, non-practicing but believe."

"Mmmm-kay. Education?"

"Bachelor of Science. I double majored in Life Sciences and Science, Technology, and Society at MIT, and I have an MS and PhD in biomedical forensics from Boston University," he told her.

"Family? Aside from the daughter?"

"Mother, father, married 35 years. Older brother...he's 31. He has a wife and two kids. An aunt and uncle in Bath...5 cousins. Grandparents are all gone, I'm afraid."

"And what's the rush?" asked her friend, getting to the real question.

"Because when she wrecked, they wouldn't let me see her or tell me anything, and I realized I don't want to spend one moment without her ever again."

CHAPTER 8

The next morning, Gideon arrived at the sheriff's office once again just before 7. He whistled as he came through the door. "Good morning, Brenda," he said, greeting his co-worker.

"Good morning," she replied. "You're in a good mood, given your girlfriend was in a wreck yesterday."

"Ayuh, because she's not my girlfriend. She's my fiancée," he announced. "I'll have invitations for you lot later in the week. But don't make plans for the 15th."

"Of this month?" Brenda gasped.

"Ayuh," he answered, whistling as he walked to his desk.

Dom shook his head. "You've lost your ever-lovin' mind."

"Ever-lovin', Dom. Those are the key words. When you know, you know. Any word on the canvasing of the cabins out by Greeleys Landing?"

"A Peaks-Kenny State Park Ranger found a recently abandoned cabin that wasn't supposed to be in use. There's evidence of three people having been chained to the furniture with handcuffs, maybe," Dom answered.

"Damn," Gideon said.

"Yeah, the State Police are taking point as of this mornin'. Mainly cuz you did your job too well yesterday, Gideon," Dom grumbled.

"I expected they would," Gideon noted. He got to work on his reports.

At 9, his mother dropped Tracey off at the office. He clocked out, and the two of them went to the municipal building to get the marriage documentation paperwork, which they filled out and signed. Then they called the clerk, making an appointment to get their marriage license at 2:30. Tracey called Mr. Hancock and asked him to officiate. He gladly accepted.

Gideon pulled into the bank parking lot and parked in a space near the door. He walked beside Tracey as they entered the bank. "Let's get you on the safe deposit box, Honey," he suggested as they approached reception. She chuckled at his eagerness.

Joanie Beachamp, from Customer Service, helped them add Tracey before she handed her a copy of the key. "Do you want to access it today?" she asked cheerily.

"Yes, please," Gideon replied before Tracey could protest.

Joanie led them into the vault. At box 1239, she inserted her key and turned it. Gideon inserted his and pulled the box free when Joanie had left the room.

He took a deep breath and grabbed Tracey's hand. "I've actually kept one secret, Baby." He opened the box.

Tracey stared at the contents, and her mouth dropped.

———

He walked into the sheriff's office to find Detective George Davison of the Maine State Police waiting at his desk. Detective Davison was in his mid to late 50s but fit and well-groomed. He obviously took pride in his appearance and took good care of his body. Brenda was practically drooling, Gideon thought.

"Deputy!" the detective greeted Gideon cordially. "I'm

Detective George Davison. I look forward to working with you on this case." He held his hand out to shake Gideon's. Gideon was confused. Dom had seniority. But he clasped the man's hand.

George seemed to read his mind. "I asked for you, Deputy."

"Oh...okay. I'm happy to help you in any way I can."

"Great! I got a room out at Peaks Kenny Lodge because I wanted to be closer to..." He looked at his notebook. "Greeleys Landing...where the bodies have been found."

"Bodies?" Gideon asked. As far as he knew, the other two women were still just missing. Then it became clear why the detective wanted him.

"Ayuh, we have evidence that Christine Richards and Becky Hawk were killed by the same perp," George said. "Don't worry, Deputy. It clears you."

Gideon smiled knowingly. "It's a woman," he said softly.

"And that is why I asked for you," George affirmed. He smacked Gideon on the back. "Come on, Kid. Take me over to the bank."

"Um...would you mind stopping at Kay Jewelers first?" Gideon asked. "I need something before I go into the bank again."

"Okay," the detective said, a quizzical expression on his face.

———

Tracey found the collar made the work very difficult. But she managed. She was a professional, and she was determined to do her job and do it well. But after just an hour, her back and her neck hurt. She leaned back into the chair and closed her eyes, trying to stretch her neck muscles a little, but that hurt worse.

"Hi, Baby," Gideon's voice said from the office door. She opened her eyes to see him standing there. God, he was gorgeous.

She couldn't help but smile. "Hi, Honey. I thought you were going back to work," she crooned, standing and stepping out from behind the desk to hug him.

"I am working," he assured her, putting his arms around her. "This is Detective George Davison with the Maine State Police. George, this is Tracey Hyun," he said, nodding to the man behind him. Detective Davison nodded and smiled. "How's your neck?" he asked Tracey.

"It hurts. But it's okay," she replied. She noticed George Davison's expression changed. He shot her the strangest look.

Gideon grinned mischievously, taking a ring box from his jacket pocket.

"Oh!" she gasped.

He snapped the box open, revealing a marquise-cut diamond ring set. He took her left hand and slipped the engagement ring onto her ring finger before kissing her. There was a round of applause from the bank employees and customers.

"I'll see you later," he whispered as he pulled away. Her heart was pounding. "I love you."

"I love you, too," she whispered back. She went back to her seat behind the desk, sat, and sighed. She no longer noticed the pain in her neck and back. She watched him approach the bank president and introduce the detective. She held up her hand to admire the ring as it sparkled like fireworks in the light.

———————

"So, tell me about the woman," George said, dipping a French fry in mayonnaise and popping it into his mouth.

"Well, the rumor mill said Becky had a new boyfriend… possibly married, since she didn't talk about him. She was supposedly seen out with him the weekend before the 4th of July. He drove a chopper. She was riding bitch," Gideon offered.

"Okay?" queried the detective.

"Becky didn't date men," Gideon hinted.

"Oh, I see. And the 'boyfriend' wore a helmet?"

"Ayuh, with a full-face visor."

"And? I know you have more than that," George laughed.

"The dress. We have a small boutique in town that sold that dress. I know because my mother bought one. My first-grade teacher is retired from teaching now, but she works part-time in the store. She described a woman who purchased three dresses, two of which were in two of the three missing women's sizes. I didn't get a size for the third, but let's assume the third dress is her size because none were in the size that fit the woman who purchased them. Plus, the store only had one in 'eggplant' to begin with, and that was the one the woman bought, and the one Becky was wearing when her body was discovered. Mrs. Kerry, my teacher, said she had never seen the woman before. She thought she might have been an out-of-stater."

"And evidence seems to indicate the women were held in a cabin in the state park," George offered.

Gideon scrunched his nose. "Ayuh, but I don't buy it. See, my fiancée was run off the road yesterday after a strange encounter with a woman who matched the description Mrs. Kerry gave me and who kind of creeped her out."

"Why did she creep her out?"

"Because she told her all the details of our relationship… as pertains to me. *I* stayed for over an hour to talk to her the night we met. *I* showed her around all day the next day. *I* moved in with her that night after my trailer burned to the ground," he extolled.

"You did? Never mind. None of my business. The point is, whoever the woman is, she is obsessed with *you*. And our first victim was *your* fiancée and the mother of *your* child. And someone tried to harm *your* current fiancée immediately after this exchange."

"Exactly. So, outsider doesn't seem quite right, but I honestly don't know anybody who matches the description. It's really weird," Gideon finished. "I assume you have DNA evidence that indicates a female perp."

"Ayuh. Under Becky Hawk's nails…and on the knife handle disposed with Christine Richards's body. What's more, the DNA matches, indicating the same female killer. Unluckily for us, it doesn't match any in the DNA database."

"So, no record," Gideon surmised.

Tracey, his mom, and Cassie came into the restaurant. He smiled and waved.

Gideon and George stood as they came over to the table. Gideon swooped up his daughter and covered her face in kisses. Cassie laughed and protested, "Daddy! Stop!"

George smiled pleasantly. "Mrs. Spencer, nice to meet you, and Miss Hyun, nice to see you again," he greeted them. "Hyun? That's Korean? Right?"

"Oh, yeah," Tracey answered, sitting next to her new

fiancé.

"And that accent...southern?" George asked.

"Richmond, Virginia," she answered with a smile. "I grew up there, but my mother was from here. Judith Ford."

"Judy...your father was Hyun Seong Min?" George sputtered. "The car? The '69 Chevy Impala SS? Black? I...I did see it!" he exclaimed, the color draining from his face. "Soo Shin! Is it you?"

"You know me, Detective? You knew my father?" she asked, confused.

He started to cry, but his tears were clearly tears of joy.

"Oh...I...well...Ayuh. I knew both of your parents, Soo Shin. I'm your Godfather," George exclaimed, gripping the table so hard his knuckles were white.

"I have a Godfather?" Tracey asked.

George laughed. "And a Godmother. Your father's sister. Hyun Hana Jin...Hannah, my wife. Ah, Jesus, Girl. We've been looking for you and your mother for years!" He jumped up and unexpectedly hugged Tracey. She was obviously taken by surprise, but she hugged him back.

CHAPTER 9

Tracey was completely flummoxed. She had been alone for so long, since her mother had died. She had no memory of her father. She'd only ever seen a picture of him. One picture. That was it. It was a professional portrait, wallet-sized, like kids got at school, of him in his Portland, Maine, Police dress uniform, taken upon his graduation from the Police Academy. And suddenly, she had a fiancé, a stepdaughter, a mother-in-law, a father-in-law, a brother-in-law, a sister-in-law, a niece, a nephew, and now an aunt and uncle, who were her Godparents!

According to her mother, Seong Min had died when Tracey was 7 months old from a brain aneurysm. He had been a Portland police officer. She had met him when her apartment had been broken into, and he was the responding officer. She never mentioned his sister or his sister's husband. After she had been widowed, she had taken Tracey to Richmond, a new city, to escape the sad memories. She had changed her name to Tracey because that was the name she had wanted to begin with. Tracey had never known she had any other family. She had even believed her mother's parents had died before she was born. Sadly, it was too late to know them now. All those years alone. And it wasn't necessary. She could have had a home. She could have had a place to go on school breaks, instead of staying at Virginia Tech alone. She could have had Christmases and Thanksgivings. She could have felt wanted and loved. But instead, she was now feeling resentment towards the mother she had adored. It was confusing.

George had quickly taken out his phone and called his wife. She had promptly proclaimed she was on her way.

Tracey just held onto Gideon's hand. She had barely eaten. It was hard to do, what with her clutching his hand like that, anyway. They had gone to get their marriage license. She released his hand long enough to sign as required and grabbed it again as soon as they were done.

Then, standing outside the bank, knowing she should go back to work, she found herself nearly hyperventilating at the thought of letting go of that strong, loving hand. He was casually leaning against his cruiser. He smiled and kissed her hand, the one with which she held onto his. And then he pulled her against him, wringing his hand from hers, and wrapping her in his protective embrace. She found her hands at his waist, her head on his shoulder.

"It's okay, my love. This is a good thing. I like him!" he chuckled.

She laughed at his reassuring words, not because they were funny or she didn't believe them, but because he filled her heart with utter joy. Thank God for her incomplete year. Thank God she had been laid off from the only job she had ever had. Thank God she'd been unable to find other employment. Thank God her grandparents left her that property. Thank God it had rained so hard she was afraid to drive in unfamiliar terrain. Thank God.

She stepped back and shouted, "I love you, Gideon James Spencer!" She spun in a circle with her hands outstretched. She would have thrown her head back, but she couldn't because of the collar.

He did, though. He threw his head back and laughed.

He stooped and picked her up around her thighs and spun, looking up at her with his gorgeous face with cheekbones like razors and that smile that extended all the way into his pretty blue eyes.

———————

Gideon and Detective Davison arrived back at the sheriff's office just before 3, thick as thieves. George followed Gideon through the door, laughing. "Rocky Raccoon? Really? That's hilarious!"

"My brother was named for the bartender on *The Love Boat*," Gideon proclaimed.

"You're making this up!" the detective howled.

"I swear to God!" he replied earnestly. "When my mom met Christine, she asked if she was named for the Stephen King novel."

"Who did she think Tracey was named for?"

"Tracey Ulman."

The detective could barely breathe; he was laughing so hard.

Dom looked up from his desk and scowled. "Having fun? Some of us are working."

"Sorry, Deputy Moretti," the detective apologized, catching his breath. "We've gotten some work done as well. I've sent for a sketch artist. Deputy Spencer has shown me the crime scenes. We've reviewed the evidence. We've spoken with the coroner…and he's offered me solid insight. Turns out he's not only a formidable investigator, but he's also a great guy. He's also marrying my niece."

"What?" Dom asked, sounding defeated somehow.

"Well, my wife's niece. Tracey's father was my brother-in-law. And my first partner on the Portland police force."

Dom huffed and shook his head.

"Everything is just handed to you on a silver platter, isn't it?" he grumbled.

"Huh?" Gideon asked.

"Nothing. Never mind." Dom slammed an open desk drawer shut and stomped off to the men's room.

"Didn't the dentist fix his tooth?" Gideon asked Brenda. She shrugged.

George looked at his watch. "It's going to be dark before we can get out to that cabin today. I'd like to take a look at it first thing in the morning," he announced, getting back to work.

"Sure. We can do that. No need to come into town first. I can come out to Peaks Kenny Lodge, and then we can make our way out there. Do you have hiking boots?"

"I need hiking boots?"

"Ayuh, you do. Come on. I'll take you to the Mercantile so you can get the appropriate gear," Gideon offered, heading back toward the door.

Dom returned as Gideon reached for the doorknob.

"Where are you going now?" Dom demanded.

Gideon grinned wickedly and said, "Shopping." Then he opened the door and stepped outside. George howled with laughter once again.

———

When Gideon entered the bank, Tracey shut down the computer, grabbing her purse. She stood and grabbed her jacket off the coat rack.

He smiled as she walked toward him, and her heart beat wildly. "Hi, Beautiful," he said, kissing her cheek.

"Back at ya," she said, grinning. He took her hand,

and they walked together out to his cruiser. He opened the passenger side door for her. She climbed inside. He shut the door and bounded around to the driver's side. Once behind the wheel, he turned to her and kissed her again, this time on the mouth and deeply. She reached up and removed the collar to allow herself to thoroughly enjoy the kiss, which took her breath away.

"My mom and dad are coming for dinner…and they invited Isaac and Janey. I'm sorry. I know you wanted to meet your aunt and talk about your father. But…Mom can be a force of nature, and she said the wedding is more important. But the good news is George said Hannah is staying a few days, so you'll have a chance tomorrow," he said apologetically as he pulled away.

Tracey laughed. She supposed most people would find the uninvited in-laws in such a situation an annoyance, but she was honestly happy. She had family. It was an amazing feeling.

"We should stop and pick up a few pizzas for dinner. No way I can cook enough for that many people," Tracey suggested.

"Oh, you don't have to cook, Baby. Mom has been making stew all afternoon," he laughed. God, this felt good. This felt normal. Tracey hadn't felt this way since before her mother died. She belonged somewhere, mostly with the man beside her. Euphoria. That was it.

He drove home, not bothering to pick up Cassie, since his parents would be coming anyway. They'd bring Cassie home.

She turned to ask if they should vacuum before their guests arrived as she walked in front of him through the front door, but he had already pulled off his jacket and started on his shirt, closing the door with his foot. He grabbed Tracey, throwing her over his shoulder and carrying her to the bedroom. She squealed, first in surprise and then in sheer delight.

Under the sweet torture of Gideon's fervent kisses and silken touch, she forgot her home was about to be filled with other people. Apparently, so did he. As he ran his hand down her side to her waist and she slipped her arms around his neck, lying back amid the pillows, pulling him down to cover her mouth with his, the doorbell rang, and they both burst into nervous laughter. "They're here," she whispered, singsongingly imitating a famous line from a movie. He buried his face in her stomach and reluctantly climbed off her, adjusting his clothing to make himself presentable. She sat up, smoothed her hair, and adjusted her skirt. "Take a cold shower, and change out of your uniform, Babe. There's no amount of adjusting that will hide it," she quipped, quickly kissing him as she headed to the door.

He nodded and undressed, acknowledging it was true.

Tracey opened the door to her new family. Cassie rushed in past her. "Take your coat off!" Tracey called to her retreating form as she ran up the stairs to her room.

"I will," she yelled as she ran. "I have to put away my new dollhouse before Sam gets here and breaks it! He said he's going to be Godzilla and smash it!" She was talking about the dollhouse that had belonged to Tracey's mom as a young girl, a beautiful Victorian, with exquisite miniature furnishings.

"Oh, God!" Tracey yelped, running to help her. "Come in! I'll be right back," she called to Nettie and Tom Spencer as she hurried up the stairs.

She and Cassie quickly got the dollhouse securely put away, and together they came back downstairs to find Gideon had showered and was building a fire in the fireplace. God, he looked great in jeans and a sweater.

The doorbell rang again, and she opened it to Isaac, Janey, and the kids. She noted that it was starting to snow, and she gasped and stepped out into the fading daylight to gaze at the first few snowflakes of a Maine winter, even though it was still technically autumn. "Oh, look," she whispered. "Pretty."

"Pretty now," Janey scoffed. "It will be a pain in the ass by morning."

Tracey smiled. "Way to burst my bubble," she laughed.

She started to go back inside as George and Hannah Davison pulled into the driveway. She smiled again and waved. The SUV barely rolled to a stop as Hannah jumped out of the passenger side and ran open-armed to Tracey.

Tracey saw her face…and knew her instantly. She felt the sob catch in her throat as she ran toward the approaching woman, calling, "Imo!" She somehow knew what she said. It was Korean. It meant father's sister.

"Jo-kah," Hannah cried, using the honorific for niece or nephew. Then, as she wrapped Tracey in her arms, she said, "My jil, my sweet baby jil," which was the informal term that indicated her brother's child.

"Bogo sip-eoyo," Tracey cried, hugging Hannah tightly. Again, she knew what she said. It was informal, "I miss you." How did she know that? She didn't speak Korean. She didn't remember her father. She didn't remember her father's sister…only…she did. He hadn't died when she was a baby. She was 5. And she did know some Korean. And she did know her aunt. And her mother had lied.

Tracey experienced a strange mix of intense grief and overwhelming joy in a flash of what could only be called an awakening. Hyun Soo Shin awoke inside Tracey's consciousness the moment she laid eyes on Hana Jin, her imo.

Hannah covered her face in kisses. Then she announced, "I made Kimchi Jjigae, Samgyeopsal, and Dolsot Bibimbap. George, bring the food." She slipped her arm through Tracey's, and they walked inside together.

"I remember," Tracey cried, holding Hannah's arm lovingly. "I remember you."

"Yes, Dear," the detective called, opening the back of the SUV.

———

"Wait...my father died of an aneurysm," Tracey interjected.

She and Hana Jin had found a moment alone together in the kitchen when they went together to get drinks for everyone. Hannah pulled out a chair at the kitchen table and sat. She motioned for Tracey to sit beside her.

"No. He was...shot. There was a burglary at an art gallery...and one of the burglars shot him...and then was shot by...George," Hannah replied haltingly. "Oh dear. I...I'm sorry, Honey. Your mother didn't handle it well. She was hospitalized for several weeks after...You stayed with George and me while she recovered. Don't you remember?"

Tracey stared with her mouth open. "I...I remember a cat...one with long white fur and blue eyes...like mine...you called her...oh...what was it? Seol-ah...That's it. I remember Halmeoni...Grandma...rocking me in her lap. I remember crying because I didn't know where my mother and father were...and you. I remember you, imo. How is it I...forgot?"

"Judy had suffered devastating depression for years. Grief at losing her husband sent her over the edge, and she just took off. As to why she lied about the circumstances of Seong Min's death, I can't really say. I think that she simply couldn't face the truth." Hannah offered, taking Tracey's hands into both of hers. "Don't blame her too harshly. It was...really hard for us all, but especially for her."

Talking to her aunt helped Tracey to forgive her mother and decide to move forward, letting the past stay in the past. Blaming her wasn't productive, and it hurt to do it. Forgiveness was the right path.

They rejoined everybody by the fireplace with drinks for everyone.

"So...what kind of wedding do you want, Tracey?" Hana Jin asked, as she took her own drink, a gin and tonic, from the tray. Hana Jin was elegant and graceful, everything that Tracey was not. Gideon's mother sighed.

Nettie was...concerned. "I'm afraid you two are moving too quickly," she suggested. "You should give it until spring at least. You've only been together for just over a month."

"No," Gideon replied softly. "I want to get married now. I know that it's fast, Mom...I do. I don't care. I know what I want."

"Gideon, I adore Tracey...but marriage isn't something you enter into on a whim," Nettie insisted. Tracey heard the apprehension in her voice as it cracked under the strain.

Gideon took Tracey's hand in his. "Trust me, Mom. We know what we're doing. This is love. Not some passing thing. I...I want to be with her...for forever. And I want forever to start now," he pleaded. Tracey sighed, loving him with her whole being. They'd never be able to explain how they were so certain about getting married. The most they could do was ask for trust.

Nettie reluctantly agreed.

They even settled upon wedding details. Nettie would clean out and decorate the large greenhouse on Drake Vale Farm. She and Janey had wanted to convert it into a wedding venue for years. Tracey would get her florist and baker to do the flowers and cake. Janey and Tracey would design simple invitations to print manually. Hannah would let Tracey wear her wedding gown. She and George had never had children of their own, and she had saved her gown in the hopes that she would someday find Tracey.

Between Nettie's beef stew and Hannah's kimchi stew, everyone was well fed and happy.

The next week was going to be very busy; that was clear.

As Tracey climbed into bed that night, her head was spinning. "You okay, Baby?" Gideon asked, pulling her close.

"Mmmm. Yeah. It's…a lot, but it's good. I never realized…no…I never admitted…how sad she was. It wasn't an accident, Gideon," she sniffed, pulling the blanket up over her. "The police ruled it an accident, but…she waited until I was 18. And then she drove into the tree she had chosen years before. I just wish I would have known how to talk to her about it."

Gideon took a deep breath. "Honey, you were just a child. 18 is…just a baby, really. She was the parent. I…I don't know what to say. I'm…just so sorry. You know, if you need to talk to someone…I…"

She laid her head on his chest. "I know I can talk to

you, Babe. But…this might require something else. I'm going to call my therapist tomorrow. It's been a while, and I'm sure I'll need to find somebody local, but I think I need a session. Don't worry. I'm not depressed. If anything, I'm happier than I've ever been. But even happiness can be overwhelming."

"Tracey…if this is too much…"

"It's not. This is what I want. All of it. All of you. Don't you know, Gideon? You and Cassie are the best thing that has ever happened to me."

They drifted off to sleep.

It was sometime around 1 am that her phone beeped. Then it rang, rousing her. She felt around the nightstand until her hand fell on the phone. She picked it up and looked at the caller ID, which read "Christine Richards."

"What the…?" she said, sitting up and staring bleary-eyed at the phone. It beeped again. She opened the text chain.

"It doesn't matter how loudly you yell you love Gideon James Spencer, or how passionately he kisses you in his police cruiser, you'll never live to be his bride," read the first text. "Die, Bitch," read the second.

"Gideon!" Tracey yelped, shaking him awake.

"What? What is it?" he asked, sitting up beside her. She handed him her phone.

CHAPTER 10

"Calm down, Kiddo," George said, laying his hand on Gideon's shoulder, as he stepped up beside him. Gideon leaned on the fence, watching the sun rise over a distant mountain.

Gideon flexed his fist half a dozen times and shook it out. "Ayuh, it wasn't very satisfying hitting the wall anyway. All I did was make a hole I have to fix."

"Not to mention, bruising your knuckles," George chided.

"What do I do?" Gideon asked, scared out of his wits, lost in a sea of conflicting emotions, and blaming himself.

"You and I solve this. We get her. We put her away. That's what you do. You do your job," George told him.

"I'm terrified. What if I'm not with her, and this bitch finds her?" Gideon implored, looking out across the snowy pasture.

"It seems like this bitch already knows where Tracey is all the time. Catching her is the best way to protect Tracey. You know that. I put a man on her, Gideon. She won't be alone. Trooper Forrest is a good man. I trust him implicitly."

Gideon nodded and turned. "Ayuh. Well. Let's get up to that cabin then." He strode toward his cruiser. George followed.

"So...she's obsessed with you," George said, as Gideon drove. "Why would she take these particular women?"

"I...I don't know. I haven't dated anyone since Christine until Tracey. I certainly wasn't interested in a middle-aged, closeted lesbian," Gideon assured the detective.

"Ayuh, I get that. But that doesn't seem to be general knowledge. How is it you knew?"

"I...I saw Becky out in Quebec City last year. She was with a woman. She saw me, and we talked. I told her I wasn't going to out her. We were friends," he replied.

"So, could anybody have misconstrued your relationship?" George asked.

"I suppose. But I don't see how. The most I ever did was shake her hand after she helped me with my financial portfolio."

"When was that?"

"Mid...June. About two weeks before she went missing. Jesus."

"What about the other two women?" George pressed.

Gideon shook his head. "It's a small community, George. I know both of them. Cassie plays with Jenny Burns all the time. They had a play date the day Hailey went missing."

"Where?"

"Oh, God," Gideon groaned. "The trailer. Hailey stayed for a cup of coffee. Then she left. She was a waitress at Bear's Den. She worked until closing. Hank picked Jenny up at 3. Hailey and Hank were separated. She'd moved back in with her mom...out by Greeleys Landing. She never made it home."

"But she was at your house that morning?"

"Ayuh, for about 15 minutes. Damn it," Gideon replied, hitting the steering wheel with both hands.

"Breathe. Grace Kemp?" George continued, speaking evenly.

"Lots of things. She's Janey's best friend." He was

crying then. Damn it, he was really turning into a crybaby.

"So, somebody could have assumed there was something between you and any of the three, though there was nothing? Right?"

"Ayuh, I guess." Gideon's heart was in his throat. "Should we postpone the wedding? God, if she gets hurt because of me…"

"Stop. That's up to you two, but whatever you decide, you're a victim, too, Gideon. It's not your fault."

Gideon nodded. "I don't know who it could possibly be, though. I swear the description…I don't know anyone like that."

"Ayuh, but she clearly knows you."

———

Tracey walked into the florist's. "Hi, Dennis. I need flowers," she announced.

"Ayuh, you've come to the right place, then," Dennis teased. He had been a good friend of her grandparents. When he had retired from the power company early, he had partnered with Yvette Ford to open this florist shop. Yvette bought him out and hired him to run it when his retirement was threatened by owning the shop. Now it belonged to Tracey. But the truth was, it was his talent and passion that fueled the business. "What ya lookin' fer, Tracey?"

"Everything," she said, sweeping her arm. "Go crazy. I'm getting married on the 15th. I want a red rose bouquet… and other than that, just make the big greenhouse at Drake Vale Farm pretty."

He stared at her for a minute. She stared back. Then he sighed. "A week and a half? I can do that."

She smiled at him. "I knew you could. Thanks. Oh.

Here's your invitation." She handed him the invitation she had printed earlier that morning.

She exited the store. Trooper Trent Forrest of the Maine State Police followed her out. "You know, you can talk to me," she quipped as she moved to the bakery next door.

"Ayuh, but I don't know anything about flowers or such," he said, smiling. "I found when I was getting married, it was best to keep my mouth shut while Tricia handled those things."

"Was it a nice wedding?"

"Ayuh, that it was," he grinned. She liked the man almost instantly. He had a great smile and a natural laugh that invited others to laugh with him.

She opened the door and entered the bakery. Willa, Dennis's wife, grinned before coming around the counter to hug and kiss the bride. "I'll make you the prettiest wedding cake you've ever seen," she proclaimed.

Gideon pushed open the cabin door. There was evidence that someone had been staying in the cabin. There were dirty dishes, ashes in the woodstove, soiled mattresses, and the smell. There were menses stains on all the bedding. There were scratches from metal on metal on the bedposts, possibly caused by restraints, but there was something off about it.

"What's wrong, Kiddo?" George asked.

"This isn't right," Gideon mused, turning and looking around. "This is how a man might hold three women...but a woman?"

"Women can be just as disgusting as men...sometimes more so," George noted.

"I don't mean the filth. But let's talk about that. Our woman bought her captives new clothes that were appropriate for the season. And a nice dress, not some tattered and worn rag. She spent $75 each on those dresses. Is she going to chain the women to beds and let them piss and shit…and bleed… all over the clothes?"

"Good point," George agreed.

Gideon pointed to a muddy boot print by the door. It was a tactical boot print, man's size 12, similar to the ones he wore, though a different brand. While Gideon wore Bates, the print appeared to be from a Danner boot. Lots of the rangers and police officers wore that brand. "That's a man's boot print, not a woman's. A man set the scene here. But it's all… faked. Look at the stains…the fluids…the pattern looks like they were poured on and spread…the pattern is unnatural."

"So…a couple?"

"I don't know, but this…I don't think Hailey, Grace, and Becky were really held here," Gideon mused.

Detective Davison nodded his agreement. "Let's get out of here, Kiddo. There's nothing more to see."

The two men made their way out of the cabin and back down the snowy trail. A mile down the trail, they met up with a couple of state park rangers on snowmobiles. They drove Gideon and George back out to Greeleys Landing Road, where Gideon had parked the squad car.

"Drop me back at Peaks Kenny Lodge," George said, getting into the passenger seat.

Gideon nodded. He didn't feel much like talking. He just kept thinking that it was all his fault…what happened to Christine…what happened to Becky. Somebody was obsessed with him and had been for a long time. And he had no clue.

What if this crazy person hurt Tracey? What would he do? Tracey. He loved Tracey. Loved her. With everything in him.

"Old girlfriends, Gideon?" George asked, breaking into his thoughts.

"Um…Like I said, no one since Christine until Tracey. Christine and I started dating after I graduated from MIT. I was 22. We lived together in Boston while I was working toward my MS and Ph.D. We lived together for 3 years. I dated a few girls in college. Nothing serious, except for…a girl I knew for 12 hours. I'd have married her. Um, then there was Chelsea Booker…I have no idea, but well…she's African American…so she really doesn't match the description. Kimberly Swanson. Um…She got married 6 years ago. Lives in Connecticut, I think. Paula Munday…a few times…She's in Boston, now. Not married, but she's been living with her current boyfriend for 3 or 4 years. Before that, I was in high school," Gideon enumerated.

"And you didn't date in high school?" George chuckled.

"No. I did. I took Marcy Henson to Senior Prom and to the movies a few times…and…well, Hailey Jones…Burns… for two years," Gideon admitted.

George was quiet for a second. "Ah. I see."

Gideon pulled into the Lodge parking lot. George got out. "I'll see you back at the office, Kiddo. Good work today. Hey, you didn't account for the girl for 12 hours…"

"She's accounted for, George. She's at the bank installing a new network."

———

Tracey worked at the bank the rest of the morning. As she shut down her computer to meet Gideon for lunch, Mr. Charleston came into the office that he had assigned her.

"How's the upgrade going, Tracey?" he asked.

"Good. I should be done by Friday," she answered, grabbing her purse.

Mr. Charleston looked nervously at Trent. "Um, will Trooper Forrest be with you all week?"

"Ayuh," the trooper answered. "Either me or another officer."

"Might I ask why?" Mr. Charleston inquired, shifting nervously on his feet.

"Without revealing any details into an ongoing investigation, suffice it to say, Miss Hyun is in need of police protection," Trent said. And that was all anybody was going to get from him. Tracey could read it on his face.

"Well…does it have anything to do with the $3,000,000 that was embezzled earlier this year?" Mr. Charleston's eyes darted back and forth between Tracey and Trent, and the bank lobby. He wrung his hands together.

"I can't say," Trent said, his face a stone mask.

"Alright, alright. Well, thank you. Enjoy your lunch." Mr. Charleston turned to leave.

"Oh, Mr. Charleston," Tracey called out, stopping him. She smiled, withdrew an invitation from her purse, and handed it to him.

———

Gideon was waiting in the parking lot. Tracey ran to his open arms, and he wrapped her up in a bear hug. Then he opened the passenger side door to his cruiser, and Tracey got in. He walked around and got in behind the steering wheel. Trent climbed dutifully into the back seat.

Gideon took a deep breath. "Tracey, Honey, about our getting married…" he started.

"Don't you dare!" she said, whirling to face him, then grabbing her neck, which was still in the collar. "Ow."

"Calm down," Gideon tried again.

"I will not. You said you wanted our forever to start right away. You can't take it back," she cried.

"I'm not trying to," he sputtered. "I'm trying to say I think we should get married right now."

"I can't believe you. I...what?"

"I think we should get married right now. We'll still have the wedding on Saturday, but we should just do it. And not tell anybody. One, we'll see how closely my stalker really is watching us. Two, I've been terrified all fucking day, and I'm done with it. If we're already married, we win," he proclaimed.

Tracey stared at him with her mouth open for a second.

And that's how it happened that Trent Forrest became Tracey's "Maid of honor." They drove directly to Mr. Hancock, who, as a member of the Maine State Bar, was a qualified wedding officiant. George stood with Gideon, and Trent stood with Tracey...a role he took a great deal of pleasure from. He kept bursting into little fits of laughter for the rest of the day. But having been sworn to secrecy, that was all. He was a man of his word.

CHAPTER 11

It started to snow again overnight. Gideon woke around 2 am and did a cursory check around the house. He didn't see any signs of anyone watching the house. The only tracks in the fresh snow were from a jackrabbit.

He checked Tracey's phone before climbing back into bed. She had no new messages from "Christine." He yawned and pulled her close as he pulled the comforter up over his head. She snuggled in against him, and he drifted off to sleep.

Moments later, he stood in his senior year dorm room at MIT. He spun around, confused for a second. The door slowly swung open, and Tracey's father, no longer wearing the garb of a Jeoseung Saja, but a Police uniform, filled the door frame.

Gideon swallowed hard. Tracey was suddenly standing beside him. She took his hand into her own. She spoke first. "Hi, Appa. I'm sorry I forgot you." She sniffed.

Her father smiled lovingly and winked. "There is nothing to be sorry for, my daughter." Turning his gaze on Gideon, he added, "Son-in-law, you need to take care of your wife. I trust you with her life."

"I...I will. I promise," Gideon swore.

"You have managed to keep the marriage a secret from the mul gwishin," Tracey's father said, "But she is an evil spirit that haunts you. You must be careful."

"What is a mul gwishin?" Gideon whispered to Tracey.

"Um...lady in white...long dark hair... drowned...like

in that movie, *The Ring*," she whispered back.

"Oh, well, that's not disturbing at all," Gideon quipped. "Why are we here?" he asked his father-in-law's spirit.

"She started here," he answered. Then he floated backwards, and the door slammed shut between them.

Both Gideon and Tracey sat bolt upright in their bed in Goose Fields Cottage. A bedside lamp lay in pieces on the floor. Sphinx meowed from the nightstand where the lamp had been. Gideon sighed in relief and picked up the cat.

———

"I don't believe it's a ghost, Tracey," Gideon said the next morning as he drove into town.

"Neither do I," Tracey replied. "I'm just sayin' it's not normal to have the same dream as someone else at the same time. There's something supernatural about it...so maybe we ought to believe Appa is telling us at least a version of the truth, as he sees it."

"Okay...okay. But the evidence indicates it started with Christine, which is here, not in Cambridge. And we have to follow the evidence. I won't discount the dream, but I need more than a shared dream and a 'drowned woman ghost' to investigate. I wouldn't even know what to investigate."

Tracey nodded.

"Can we, just for today, focus on the description of the woman at Shaw's?" he asked, squeezing her hand. "The sketch artist arrived this morning."

"Yeah. I'll do my best, Sweetheart," Tracey replied with a smile.

"Pardon me," Trent said from the backseat, "but what the hell are you talking about?"

"Jesus!" Gideon yelped. "I kind of forgot he was back

there."

They both laughed, and Trent just looked perplexed. Gideon parked, and they all walked into the sheriff's office. Brenda was just sitting down at her desk, and Dom had not yet arrived. George was waiting at Gideon's desk with the sketch artist.

"Tracey, Sweetheart, this is Fred Wilcox. He's going to walk you through the process, so no need to be nervous. He's been doing this for twenty years. Okay?" George said, introducing the sketch artist just as his phone rang. He held up one finger and answered the call. "Davison. Ayuh. I see. Please. Ayuh, send the link. Thanks." He disconnected. "Oh, damn," he said. "We got an out of state DNA match on a cold case for our perp. A Jane Doe fished out of the Charles back in 2018. Our perp's DNA matches DNA found under the Jane Doe's fingernails."

"So, she's killed someone before Christine?" Gideon asked.

George sat down at Gideon's desk and opened his laptop. He opened a file that had been forwarded to him, including pictures of the Jane Doe.

Gideon leaned over his shoulder to see.

"Fuck!" he yelled when George opened the photo. Gideon stumbled backwards, with his hand over his mouth.

"What?" George asked.

The picture of the corpse of a beautiful African American young woman with long braids and a heart-shaped face filled the screen.

"That's Chelsea Booker," Gideon answered, lowering his hand.

"The girl you dated in college, you didn't know where

she was now?" George asked.

"I was thinking suspects...not more victims!" he cried. "Oh, God."

The room fell silent. Dom came through the door. "Morning," he said. When no one returned his salutation, he asked, "What's going on?"

"That means that Christine is the second victim. Chelsea was the first," George extolled. "You're certain about the other girls' whereabouts?"

"Ayuh," Gideon muttered. "Marcy Henson works at the County Clerk's office. And the other two in college...I only know their whereabouts through the grapevine, but I'm fairly certain. We should check, though." He sighed heavily and shook his head. "How? How could someone be this fixated on me, and I not know it?" His heart was breaking. Chelsea had been a nice girl. She had grown up in foster care, so it wasn't surprising she had remained a Jane Doe for 7 years. But she had dreams, big dreams. She had been studying engineering and was interested in robotics. This was so unfair.

Tracey's arms fell around his neck and pulled him close. He held her in his arms.

Dom looked at the computer screen. "I don't get it. I mean, he's an okay-lookin' guy, but he's a rural county deputy. It's not like he's Brad Pitt or Chris Hemsworth. He makes a modest living. Heck, he lived in a trailer, for Pete's sake. What's there for anybody to get obsessed about?" Then he winked at Gideon.

"Exactly," Gideon laughed sadly. "I'm really not special."

Tracey closed her arms around his neck tighter. "You are absolutely special, my darling."

———————

Mrs. Kerry came in after Tracey sat with the sketch artist. While their description and resulting sketches were not identical, they were extremely close...close enough that it could be presumed they were describing the same woman; a Caucasian female, between 5′5″ and 5′7″ tall, weighing between 180 and 210 pounds, with a round, chubby face, shoulder length dark brown hair, an olive complexion, thin lips, a Grecian nose, and large, brown, round eyes. She was probably in her late 20s. The one thing both women agreed upon 100% was that she was missing her right top canine tooth. Gideon stared at Tracey's, Mrs. Kerry's, and the composite of both. He did not know this woman. He was certain. He asked himself over and over, who the hell was she?

He closed his eyes. Hyun Seung Min had said it had started in his dorm room. What with Chelsea's murder 7 years before, that tracked. Maybe his roommate could help. He took out his phone and called Scott Unger.

He got voicemail. So, he left his name and number and turned back to the sketches. Drowned ghost, he thought. Drowned ghost. He googled drownings in Cambridge in 2017-18. Nothing matched. Drowned...drowned...drowned.

The hazing incident!

He picked up the composite sketch...fifty pounds lighter, and that could be the girl. "Fred!" he called out, louder than he'd intended. "Can you show me this person 7 years younger and 50 pounds lighter?"

"What are you thinking?" George asked him.

"Graduation week, in my dormitory, there was a hazing incident. A girl was forced into the showers and stripped while being held under a cold spray. It happened to be on my floor, and I…kinda of punched the weasel of a guy who was the ringleader while a couple of girls covered up the girl. I held the guy down until campus police arrived. I didn't know the girl…and I was moving out, so I never knew who she was," he explained. "Later, I called to check on her, and I was told that she was fine, but they wouldn't release any information."

As he spoke, Fred drew. He held up the new sketch. "That's her. That's the girl," Gideon exclaimed.

———

Gideon walked back to his desk to find a man waiting for him. The man, who had been seated in the chair beside his desk, stood as Gideon approached.

"Deputy Gideon Spencer?" the man asked, outstretching his hand for Gideon to shake.

Gideon grasped his hand firmly. "Yes," he replied.

"I'm Ben Young, with National Fidelity…I'm your claims adjuster," the man replied with a cold smile.

"Oh…yes…Mr. Young. Please…have a seat," Gideon offered, sitting behind his desk.

"I'm afraid there's an issue with your claim, Mr. Spencer," Ben Young advised him. "It seems the fire marshal has ruled the fire's cause as arson. We have to wonder if you were involved," the strange little man sneered.

"You're kidding me?" Gideon huffed, burying his head in his hand. "Why on Earth would I do that?"

"Maybe you needed the money," Mr. Young offered.

Gideon laughed in his face.

"Pay me or not. Of course, should you not, then I'll sue. I assure you I'll win. Yes, the fire was caused by arson. It doesn't take a genius to figure that out. The smell of gasoline at the scene was obvious. I was otherwise…occupied…at the time. I have a stalker, Mr. Young. It's well-documented and the focus of a joint investigation between the Piscataquis County Sheriff's Department and the Maine State Police. I have no motive to burn everything I own. I don't need money. My policy covers arson, as long as I am not the arsonist. I believe I can be cleared of that. So do what you have to, and cut the damn check," Gideon snarled, his eyes narrowing as he leaned closer to Mr. Young. His jaw was tight.

Mr. Young leaned back further and further as Gideon spoke.

"I'll…I'll let you know in a few days, Mr. Spencer," he stammered when Gideon had finished. He grabbed his briefcase, hugged it to his chest, stumbled out of the chair, and practically ran out of the office.

Gideon shook his head and blew out a long breath.

"Everything okay?" George asked, as he walked over to Gideon's desk, watching the insurance man depart.

"Ayuh, it will be fine. They'll pay. I just have to prove I didn't burn down my own home. What an asshole," he chuckled.

George snorted and slapped Gideon on the back. "Never met an insurance adjuster who wasn't an asshole," he quipped. "You think your stalker did it?"

"Who else?" Gideon replied.

George nodded.

CHAPTER 12

Tracey worked the rest of the morning. Just before lunch, Dom came into the bank to make a deposit. She smiled and waved. He nodded in recognition of her greeting. She thought for a second, then made up her mind. Gruff as he may be, Dom worked with Gideon, and she wanted to be on good terms with Gideon's friends. She stood and left her desk, walking over to Dom.

"Hey, Dom," she said, standing next to him.

"Oh, hey, Tracey," he responded, looking surprised. "What can I do for you?"

"Nothing. I was just wondering what you were doing for lunch," she suggested. "If you don't have plans, maybe we could get to know each other a little better." She smiled.

"I...uh...aren't you marrying Gideon?"

"Ewww. Yes, I'm marrying Gideon. I just thought we could be friends," she protested.

"Oh. I'm sorry. I just wasn't expecting that. Sure. Lunch. Why not?"

She went back to her desk, shut down the computer, and grabbed her purse and coat. Trent followed as Tracey and Dom headed out. "Pizza?" Tracey asked.

"Eh, I'm not a fan of the local pizza. I'm from Jersey. You can't get pizza here as good as in Jersey," Dom replied. "Same goes for the Chinese. Bear's Den is good."

"Sure," Tracey agreed. They got into his squad car, Trent in the back. "So, you're originally from New Jersey?"

"Hmmm, yeah. Trenton. I moved here 4 years ago. I was looking for a change. I saw an ad for a deputy position and thought country life sounded...idyllic. Know what I mean?" He laughed.

"Oh, yeah. I've been enjoying it. But this is really different from Trenton...wow. You must have gone through some culture shock!" Tracey chuckled.

"Sure, some. But I like it here."

Tracey stifled her laugh. He was always grumpy... if this was his liking something, she didn't want to see him disliking it.

He parked, and they got out of the car. They walked across the parking lot. Trent followed quietly. Inside, they grabbed a table and ordered burgers and fries. As they ate, Tracey pushed for more information about Dom. She was determined to break through that gruff exterior.

"So, do you miss your family?" she asked as the waitress placed their food in front of them.

"Nah. It's just me. My pops passed away a while ago," he replied, falling silent again. It was like pulling teeth. "I'm not that close to my ma. We haven't spoken in years."

"You said you moved here 4 years ago? That's when Gideon started with the sheriff's department, too. Were you guys hired together?"

"Oh, no. I started 3 months before Gideon. He took a few months off after graduating college. I think he actually had a job lined up in Boston. Not sure what made him choose to stay here after..." He fell silent again.

"Oh...I see. Where did you go to school?" she tried again.

"Me? No. I joined the Navy out of high school." Again,

he didn't elaborate.

"Um...hey, we should go out on a double date sometime. Me and Gideon...you and...whoever you are seeing. What kind of movies do you like?" she suggested.

"Oh...I've gone out a few times with Charity Howe from church. We could do that. She likes those rom-com chick flicks. I imagine you do, too."

"Ah. Charity...Howe? I don't think I've met her yet."

"Well, she's Catholic," he replied, as if that explained why Tracey hadn't met her.

She looked imploringly at Trent. He just shrugged.

Janey Spencer came in as she was finishing her burger. Tracey waved and said to Dom, "Oh, you know, I need to talk to Janey about the wedding. I'll just catch a ride with her."

"Sounds good," he replied. "See you around. Thanks for lunch." He got up and left.

"I guess I'm buying," she said to Trent, incredulously. Trent smiled. "Oh, shut up," she teased. He chuckled quietly.

Janey made her way over. "You had lunch with the sour puss? How'd that go?" she asked, laughing.

"Weirdly," Tracey answered, and they both laughed.

Gideon dug through the box he had pulled out of his childhood room closet, finding his senior yearbook from MIT. He shoved everything he'd pulled out back in and put the box back on the top shelf in the closet. He grabbed the yearbook and bounded back downstairs.

"Find what you were looking for?" his mother asked.

"Ayuh, got it," he said, kissing her cheek.

"Can I go with you, Daddy?" his daughter asked from the sofa, where she sat playing with a doll.

"No, Babydoll, Daddy's working. And you're staying with Granny and Grandaddy tonight, remember?" He had arranged for his parents to keep Cassie overnight so he and Tracey could have a romantic evening. He'd replaced the steaks and lobsters from the other night, when she had been run off the road. "Jenny Burns is going to spend the night. Remember?"

"Oh!" Cassie exclaimed excitedly. "I forgot." She giggled and was so darned cute. Gideon scooped her up and kissed her.

"I love you, Cassie," he assured her.

"I love you, too, Daddy," she replied. He dropped her back onto the sofa, and she squealed with delight as she fell.

"Oops. I couldn't hold on," he teased. "Have fun, Babydoll. Thanks, Mom. I gotta get back." With that, he headed out.

As he drove past the Bear's Den, he saw Dom getting into his cruiser, and he honked and waved. Dom looked up and nodded.

Back at the office, he sat at his desk and looked through the yearbook, slowly, scanning each picture. Finally, he found her. Class of 2020, physics major. Her name was Lisa Biacchi. He grabbed the alumni directory and found her listing. He called the number listed. When the voicemail message started, his eyes grew large, and he choked on the coffee he was drinking.

He waved George and the sheriff over. He disconnected and recalled the number, placing the call on speaker and recording it.

"Hello, it's Lisa. Sorry, but I'm out of town. It's finally happening! My fiancé, Gideon Spencer, and I are finally tying the knot on the 15th. Leave a message after the beep, and *we'll* get back to yous when we get back," the woman's voice said.

"Jesus," the sheriff said.

Dom came in the door. "We have a suspect," Gideon said, playing the recording.

"That's nuts," Dom agreed, sitting at his desk.

Brenda took a call. "Mrs. Gray, out at Spruce Brook Farm, says she saw a prowler out in her barn."

"I'll go," Dom said, sighing. "It's been a whole month since she's seen a prowler," he joked.

He walked out but was back minutes later. "Damned battery died. Can I take your cruiser, Gideon?"

"Um. Sure," Gideon replied, tossing him his keys.

Dom pulled on a balaclava as he walked back out. "It's starting to snow again," he noted.

———

Tracey took the rest of the afternoon off. She was ahead of schedule and wanted to spend some time with Janey. They talked to the owner of The Bear's Den about catering the wedding and decided on the menu. They went to the Mercantile and bought some decorations, ribbon, tealight candles, and a ton of mason jars.

Back at Goose Fields Cottage, Janey and Tracey tied ribbons around the tops of the mason jars and dropped a tealight candle into each one.

"You guys sure you aren't rushing things?" Janey asked as she tied a ribbon.

Tracey smiled. "We are rushing things. We both know that. But we both know we want to be together, and it's a forever thing. I know it sounds crazy," she explained. "The truth is…I've been alone nearly a third of my life, Janey. And for nearly two-thirds, it was just me and my mom. But the second I met Gideon...I wasn't alone anymore. I fell in love with him at first sight. I really did. Maybe it's a mistake. But I'm goin' to make it if it is."

"Well...I wish you all the best, Tracey. Gideon...he's been hurt, too. When Christine disappeared, he just shut down. And he's more like himself than he's been in years since meeting you. I'm not trying to discourage you. I just want to make sure you guys know what you're doing," Janey said. Tracey could see the earnestness on her face. Janey cared about Gideon. She didn't want to see him hurt.

"I love him. Completely. I feel like I've known him forever," Tracey assured her.

"Would you mind...a little test?" Janey asked, laughing.

"Not at all."

"How does he take his coffee?" Janey asked.

"Black, two sugars."

"What's his favorite meal?"

"Thanksgiving." Tracey laughed. "But only on Thanksgiving. He loves family gatherings."

"Favorite ice cream?"

"Moose Tracks."

"Besides Christine, his biggest regret?"

"Never learning to play the piano," Tracey guffawed.

Janey burst out laughing. "Not bad. Not bad."

"Thank you very much," Tracey replied, bowing. She checked the time on her phone. "Oh, I should start the lobsters," she proclaimed. The phone rang in her hand. She accepted the call. "Hey, Baby. I was about to start the lobster. What? Oh my God! Wait, why do you think that? Oh. I see. I'll just give the lobsters and steaks to Janey. I understand. I love you, too. Please be careful. Yeah. Trent is here. He's standing guard outside. Yeah, I'll let him in. I'll see you when you get home. Bye, Honey." She looked at Janey as she disconnected. "Dom went out on a call in Gideon's cruiser, wearing a ski mask. He never showed up at the call. They found the cruiser at Greeleys Landing. There was blood. Lots of blood. They think someone took Dom, thinking it was Gideon. He's working late to help with the search." A sob escaped her throat as she spoke. Janey rubbed her back.

"He'll be okay, Trace. He's a good deputy. He really is," she assured her.

Tracey sniffed and nodded. "I know. But it's still… really scary," she cried, burying her eyes in her hand.

CHAPTER 13

Trent stood as Gideon came through the door. Gideon waved as he stooped to take off his boots, which he left by the door. "Hey, Trent. Go on back to the Lodge. Get some sleep," he whispered.

"Oh, geez. What time is it?" Trent asked, stretching.

"Just after midnight," Gideon answered. "Thanks for staying with Tracey."

"Oh, you bet. If it were Tricia, I'd want someone to stay, so I don't mind. Did you guys find him?"

Gideon shook his head solemnly. "No. No tracks in the snow leading away from the car. I...I think it was pushed from the blacktop and let to roll to a stop after whoever was in it got out. I think that's how they did it with the women, too. No tracks on the blacktop. The rain washed them away last spring and summer...and the snowplow got rid of them in the snow. The thing I don't understand is why the dogs didn't hit on anybody. In the spring, they just came back to us. And tonight, they kept coming back to me...probably because it was my car. I finally had to leave in hopes they'd hit on a scent other than mine."

Trent nodded. "Well, I'll see ya in the morning then. G'night."

"Night."

Trent headed out the door.

Gideon poked the fire and closed the doors on it. It would die before morning. He smiled at the dozens of mason jars his beautiful wife had prepared.

It appeared that his stalker did not know he and Tracey had already gotten married, but something had instigated the "attack," for lack of a better word now, on Dom. Maybe his calling Lisa Biacchi's home phone had pushed her to make a move.

Whatever had been the impetus, Gideon felt an immense amount of guilt over it. Dom wasn't the friendliest guy, but they had worked together for nearly 4 years. It killed him that something had happened to Dom in his stead.

He turned off the light and went into the bedroom where Tracey was sleeping soundly. He quietly undressed, pulled on his pajama bottoms, and climbed into bed beside her. She moaned softly, and he wrapped his arms around her, pulling her close. She instinctively threw her leg over him and snuggled her face against his neck, her warm breath mingling with his. His mouth sought out hers, and they kissed.

It was around 2:30 when the car pulled into the driveway. Gideon was awakened by the rapping on the front door. He grabbed his weapon from the gun safe and went to peer through the front window.

A couple stood on the front porch. The woman had long blonde hair, the man, shoulder-length brown hair, and a goatee and mustache. "Tracey! Trace! It's Gigi and Cal," the woman called, laughing and rapping on the door again.

"Gigi!" Tracey exclaimed from the bedroom door.

Gideon lowered his weapon and sighed in relief. He flipped on the light and opened the door, still shirtless.

"Do you know what time it is?" he scolded them, waving them inside with the weapon.

"Whoa," the man named Cal squeaked, seeing the gun.

"What are you guys doing here?" Tracey squealed excitedly, rushing forward to hug them.

"You said you're getting married. We came to help with your wedding," Gigi answered, hugging Tracey. They both started jumping up and down, and Gideon walked back to the bedroom to return the weapon to the gun safe and pull on a T-shirt.

He came back into the living room to find their guests sitting on the sofa. He opened the fireplace door and threw in two more logs before turning to speak to them. "Hi, I'm Gideon," he said.

"We figured," Gigi said, smiling and offering her hand. He shook it.

"What's with the gun?" Cal asked, accusatory tones dripping in his voice.

"It's the middle of the night, and I don't know you," Gideon responded.

"So, you shoot people you don't know?"

"Are you shot?" Gideon derided.

"Hush, Cal. He's a cop. It's normal he'd have a gun," Gigi informed her boyfriend, laying her hand on his knee.

"Oh. I didn't know that. You didn't tell me that," Cal complained. "All brawn and no brain."

"I have a double major BS in Life Sciences and Science, Technology, and Society from MIT, and a master's and a Ph.D. in Biomedical Forensic Science from Boston University."

"Oh," said Cal.

"Where's Tracey?" Gideon asked, ignoring the disdain in Cal's voice and face.

"Getting hot chocolate. It's freakin' cold outside," Gigi responded.

Tracey appeared from the kitchen, and the front door burst open. She screamed as Isaac and Tom ran inside, lowering their shotguns at her friends.

"Put those away," Gideon laughed. "These are Tracey's college friends, Gigi and Cal."

"Are they cops, too?" Cal asked, grabbing his chest.

"No, they're my dad and brother being overprotective," Gideon said.

———

After they got Gigi and Cal set up on the sleeper sofa in Tracey's home office for the night, and Isaac and Tom were sent home, Tracey lay beside Gideon. "You're going to be beat tomorrow," she whispered, snuggling against him.

"Hmmm, no. I can sleep in. I've been removed from the investigation. I'm a victim now," he told her. "You are supposed to work, though."

"Yeah, but I am ready to upload the system. All I have to do is push a button, basically. And then be there for the inevitable questions and user errors. I'll be fine." She sighed deeply and closed her eyes. "I love you."

"Mmmm, I love you, too," he mumbled as they finally fell asleep.

A short two and a half hours later, when the alarm went off, Tracey climbed out of bed, showered, dressed, and applied her makeup before she opened the front door to Trent Forrest.

"Good morning, Trent," she said, smiling broadly.

"Miss Hyun," Trent greeted her.

"Oh, come on! You were my maid of honor! A little enthusiasm," she teased.

"What?" Gigi exclaimed from the stairs. "You're

already married? And this…guy…was your maid of honor?"

Tracey grimaced. Trent chuckled.

"Um…yeah, and yeah," she answered. "But that's a secret, Gigi. Can you keep it quiet? We're still having the wedding."

"I don't get it. What is your rush? You couldn't even wait two weeks?"

Tracey looked at her friend and knew she'd have to explain. She didn't know if she could, though. It was true what she'd said to Janey. It had been love at first sight. Only first sight hadn't been a month ago.

"Gigi, remember the college tour trip to Boston senior year of high school?"

"Of course. We visited Harvard, MIT, and Boston University. You nearly missed the bus back to Richmond. And when you got on the bus, you said you were madly in love. Kind of my point. You fall in love easily."

"That was Gideon," Tracey said quietly. She smiled sweetly. "I've only ever loved Gideon. No one else."

————

Gideon had dreamed of the beautiful girl he'd spent 12 hours with on one fall day 10 years ago for many years. He had been dreaming of her for more than 10 years, truth be told. It had been one of the things that he and Christine had fought about. Christine insisted he would leave her for the girl if he ever saw her again. He insisted that he was committed to Christine and Cassie, regardless of the recurring dream. He wondered now if that were true. Because the second he saw her again, he was hers. Maybe Christine had been right after all.

In the dream, Tracey was sitting on the grass beside

Sebec Lake. Why, he didn't know. He hadn't known she was the Fords' granddaughter. As far as he knew, she had no ties to his home. But for 10 years, they met in dreams on the shore of Sebec Lake, and she was sitting in the grass, out by Steadman Landing, past Orca Rock, near where Cotton Brook emptied into the lake. And that was it. There was nothing erotic about it…at first. They sat on the grass and talked about their lives. And he grew to love her more with every encounter. She talked about her mother's death and about going to Virginia Tech. As the years passed, she told him about her job with the Marketing firm. She laughed about how her friend Gigi was dating a vegan, and how hard it was for Gigi to hide her love for cheeseburgers. Mostly, she told him that she was waiting for him. He told her everything, too.

He finally gave up on going back to sleep. He got up and went into the kitchen. Gigi was sitting at the table drinking a cup of coffee. "Good morning," he greeted her.

"Good morning," she replied. She was dubious of him, he could tell.

"I'm going to make some eggs and bacon. Want some? Or is Cal the vegan you hide you eat meat from?" he asked, without thinking.

"No, that was Austin. How do you know that?" she asked.

He stared at her for a second. "What are your thoughts on Carl Jung and synchronicity?" he asked.

"In regard to what?"

"Dreams…more specifically…shared dreams," he replied, pouring himself a cup of coffee.

"A shared consciousness? I think I believe Freud," Gigi, who had majored in psychology, answered.

"Hmmm. I used to agree," he said cryptically. "Scientific support for such an occurrence would be nearly impossible to generate. And yet..."

"Do you think you've shared dreams with somebody?" Gigi scoffed.

He smiled and sat across from her. "Your name is Georgia Glynn Winston. But you hate it because it is too close to Glamorous Glennis, so you prefer Gigi. You've known Tracey since you were 10, when you moved from Memphis to Richmond. You've been best friends since you were 11, when you and she were invited to Tiffany Martin's birthday party, but as a joke. She shoved the bitch into the pool. You say she falls in love easily, but she's only ever said she was in love once. She's dated but never fallen in love. You, on the other hand, fall in love often, starting with Ricky Long in 8th grade, right up to Cal...Calvin Johnson...who you may actually really be in love with."

"You two have nothing better to talk about than me?" Gigi huffed.

"Other than when you called, we haven't talked about you once. In my dreams, over the last 10 years, she talks about you often," he said. "Eggs?"

"Sure. I could eat," Gigi responded, admitting defeat by dropping it.

As he served her a plate full of bacon and eggs, she asked, "Where are you in these dreams?"

"Out by Sebec Lake, past Orca Rock, near the mouth of Cotton Brook," he replied, setting his own plate on the table.

"Tracey's birthday is on the 26th. Her mom...died on..."

"The 27th. I know. It was the day after Thanksgiving. This year it falls on Thanksgiving."

"Did she share that in a dream?" Gigi laughed.

"Ayuh, she did. The night after it happened. She cried. I held her. At least in the dream."

———

Tracey finished her job early but stayed until closing to put out proverbial fires as they broke out. Human error was high during a rollout of a new network. That was just a fact of life. It went relatively smoothly, though.

For lunch, she met her Aunt Hannah at Moon Hing Chinese Restaurant. "I brought my wedding gown," she said excitedly. "I hope you like it, Tracey."

"Awesome. My best friend Gigi showed up last night. We can try it on at the cottage this evening. We'll make it a girls' night. Are you staying tonight?"

"I planned on it. I told Nettie I'd help clean the greenhouse this weekend," she agreed.

Trent smiled. "Do I get a pretty dress, too, Tracey?" he whispered when Hannah got up to use the restroom.

"You bet," she chuckled.

When Hannah returned, they paid their check and left, Trent and Tracey going back to the bank, and Hannah heading out to Peaks Kenny Lodge, where her husband was staying throughout this investigation.

———

Gideon headed out to the sheep barn to help his brother feed the sheep. Cal followed him at Gigi's suggestion. "So, what exactly do you do with the sheep?" Cal asked, trying desperately to keep up with Gideon, who was taller and in better physical condition than the hipster Cal.

"We shear them in the spring, for the wool. Some are sent to the slaughterhouse. And the ewes are milked," Gideon answered.

"Shearing is inhumane," Cal complained.

"Not shearing is worse," Gideon huffed.

"How can you kill animals you raise?" Cal continued.

"I don't. My brother is the farmer. I'm just helping him out on my day off, forced as it may be," Gideon retorted.

"But you grew up on a farm?"

Gideon stopped walking. "Ayuh. So?"

"I mean…you would know better than I about how… someone can kill an animal they raise," Cal sputtered.

"Well, I suppose it's because the animals aren't pets. They're livestock. I wouldn't kill my cat. He's a pain in the ass, but he's still my cat," Gideon said, exasperated.

"I don't really understand the difference," Cal interjected.

"Well, then, I don't suggest farming as a career for you," Gideon chuckled. "You really aren't the vegan?"

"What? No, I eat some meat."

"If I were you, I'd try not to think about where that meat comes from," Gideon told him.

In the sheep barn, Isaac was filling troughs with hay. "Cal came to help," Gideon said with a grin.

"Oh. Okay. Well, start by mucking out the pens," Isaac suggested.

Gideon pulled on a set of muck-encrusted rubbers. "You'll need a pair of these," he laughed.

"Oh. Oh my," Cal exclaimed, retching as he pulled on the set of rubbers next to the ones Gideon had grabbed.

————*

Tracey was available for the bank employees the rest of the afternoon and promised to be in-house the next day and all next week before packing up to leave for the day. She shut down her computer to find Gideon, dressed in jeans and a sweater, waiting for her by his truck.

"Hey, Babe," he greeted her, giving her a quick kiss on the lips, which he had to stoop to give because of the collar. "I know. I know. Girls' night. As long as Trent is there, I'm fine with it, but I wanted to talk, so I thought I'd waste our precious natural resources and drive you home before going over to Mom and Dad's with Cal. He's a peach, by the way."

She laughed. "He's an acquired taste."

He helped her into the truck and walked around to the driver's side. He climbed in himself and started the engine.

"I met with the adjuster about my trailer yesterday. They are investigating my claim. It was arson. Naturally, they think I did it," he scorned. "I should get used to people finding me suspicious, I suppose. Lord knows Gigi does."

Tracey sighed. Of course. Gigi. "I'll try to get her to understand. She's a pragmatist," Tracey said.

"Ayuh, that she is. I thought since she was a psychology major, she'd understand the Jungian connection, but she can't really grasp the shared dreams thing," he said.

Tracey sat there for a minute. She'd never mentioned Gigi's major...when awake.

"They were real. All of them. Hundreds of dreams. 10 years of friendship, of loving you. We'll never get anybody else to understand it. And we don't have to. We know," she said quietly, just above a whisper.

"I only know, I know everything about you, and you know everything about me. I can't think of any other explanation. I've met you hundreds of times out by the lake."

"On a grassy spot on a gingham blanket," she added.

"I held you when your mother died."

"I held you when Christine disappeared."

"You celebrated Cassie's birth with me."

"You encouraged me when I was laid off."

"That's why I asked you to marry me. That's why you said yes. Because we have known each other and loved each other for a long time," he whispered back to her.

"We decide. Not them. Okay?" she assured him. It was real. Whatever it was, a psychic connection, a Jungian synchronicity, a mystic shared dream, or something else, it bonded them together.

He took her hand in his. "I love you, Tracey. That's all that matters. Anything else outside of that…the money, the insurance, suspicions about me, some woman I don't even know being obsessed with me…I can face it all…because I have you. I just want you to know that."

Tracey grinned and bit her bottom lip. "Back at ya," she giggled.

He kissed her again, having to maneuver his head in front of her, due to the collar. "I can't wait for that thing to go away," he laughed.

CHAPTER 14

Tracey entered her home, the first place that had ever felt like a home to her. Her friend Gigi had done some cleaning while she had been at work. The cottage practically sparkled.

"Wow. This place looks great!" Tracey proclaimed. "Want a job?" she teased.

"Ha!" Gigi responded. "You've got some pretty valuable antiques here. Did you know?"

"I figured. The cottage...at least the living room and bedroom portion, was built in 1789. Apparently, my grandfather's family has owned this land continuously since before the Revolutionary War."

"That's quite a heritage," Gigi acknowledged.

"I suppose. It's sad. My mother cut off all ties to any past. And she didn't just choose that for herself, but for me, too. And not just her family, but my father's, as well. He left her that Impala. And she left it to me. That and one old photograph were the only ties I had to the past. Now...I have this beautiful place to live, with all these lovely things that her family owned for centuries in some cases. And did I tell you? I have an aunt. My father's sister. And I remember her, Gigi. And when I saw her, I remembered him...Appa...Daddy. I was 5 when he died, not a baby," Tracey said, kicking off her shoes and flopping down onto the sofa. "Come on in, Trent. Don't stand in the door."

Trent nodded and entered.

"And your own personal shadow," Gigi laughed,

waving to the policeman.

"Trent's cool. He and his wife are expecting their first baby in April. A girl, Trent?" Tracey asked, motioning for him to take a seat.

He dutifully chose a seat with a clear sight line to the door.

"Ayuh, Madeline Ophelia. Tricia has a flair for the dramatic," he smiled.

"It's a very pretty name," Tracey noted, putting her feet up on the coffee table. "When I have a baby, I think I'll choose names that remind my child of their heritage. Like Hana Judith for a girl or Gideon Min for a boy. I like having roots, you know."

"Well, you certainly look contented. I'll give you that," Gigi laughed.

The doorbell rang. Trent stood and strode to the door. He opened it to Hana Jin, who had a garment bag in her arms. George Davison was behind her with a box full of tacos from a local Mexican restaurant called Fiesta Wey, a bottle of tequila, a bottle of Margarita mix, and a bag of ice.

"Ahhh! A man after my heart!" Gigi squealed, taking the bottles from him.

Tracey made the introductions before George kissed his wife and left.

Moments later, Nettie, carrying Vivi, and Janey came in together, with Cassie and Sam, while Gigi was blending the margaritas. Tracey noticed Gigi didn't put any tequila into her own drink but said nothing. Cassie ran to Tracey and hugged her, climbing onto her lap.

"You're my mommy now, right?" she asked earnestly.

"You bet," Tracey replied, hugging her. "Why?"

"Jenny Burns told her you weren't her real mommy, just like Jessica Charleston isn't hers. Apparently, Hank has started dating again," Janey whispered behind her hand, trying to hold onto Sam's hand.

"Oh, I see. Well, Cassie, my love, I would be happy to be your real mommy...and if you want it, we can make that happen," Tracey assured her with a kiss.

"How?" Cassie asked, cocking her head.

"Adoption," Tracey replied, poking her in the belly button.

Cassie slung her arms around Tracey's neck in excitement. It hurt, but that didn't matter. She wrapped her arms around the child and squeezed.

"Can we go play now?" Sam pleaded.

"Ayuh, scoot," Janey replied, smacking his butt as he ran for the stairs. Cassie yelped and jumped off Tracey, following her cousin.

————

Gideon took a sip of his pilsner, watching his brother and Cal as they played pool. Cal was a tool. He hadn't changed his mind about that, but for a hipster, he did at least put in an effort on the farm today, and he was relatively funny. He and Isaac seemed to be having a lot of fun together. He laughed when Isaac scratched. "Ewwww. Scrrrrraaaatchhhh," Cal teased.

"Watch it, little man, or I'll let the ram loose on ya," Isaac returned, laughing.

"I may be little, but I kick your giant ass at pool," Cal quipped, opening his mouth in a mock shock expression.

"He has beaten you 4 times in a row," Gideon guffawed.

"Then you play him," Isaac retorted.

"Nope. I recognize a hustler when I see one," Gideon laughed, as their father, Tom, and George came down the basement stairs to join them in the mancave.

"Oh, this is nice," George said, admiring the Patriots themed décor. "Hey, I saw a moose outside." He pointed up the stairs.

"It's Maine. That'll happen," Isaac observed.

"A moose? Really?" Cal sounded excited. "I've never seen a moose."

"Well, we can go take a look, Cal, but keep your distance. Moose are mean as shit," Isaac told his new friend.

"Really?"

"I'd rather a bear in town than a moose," Gideon agreed. "Bears are more afraid of humans. Moose are just assholes."

Cal laughed. "Okay, I'll take your word for it, but I'd still like to see it." He chuckled as he followed Isaac and Gideon up the stairs. "Moose are just assholes. That's funny. Marty Moose from 'Vacation'? Remember that old movie? That moose was definitely an asshole."

All three of the younger men laughed. George looked at Tom. "Well, we know how to clear a room."

"Ayuh. It's a talent that comes with age."

Outside on the back deck, Gideon pointed out past the back pasture near the tree line. "There he is. He's a big one."

"Ayuh," Cal said, imitating their accent. "That moose is a moose, alright."

Gideon couldn't help it. He laughed. He leaned his head between his arms on the deck railing and laughed.

He felt the bullet fly past his head as it hit the porch light, and the deck went dark. He yelped and hit the ground.

"Get down!" he yelled, pulling Cal down with him. Issac wasn't as fast. A second bullet hit him in the thigh, and he fell. Gideon shoved Cal back into the house, grabbed Isaac's collar, and pulled him inside with him as he crawled through the door. He slammed the door and yelled. "Sniper! Isaac's hit! Call 911." He pulled off his own belt and tightened it around his brother's leg.

"Owwwww!" Isaac screamed as the belt cut into his leg.

"I'm sorry. I'm sorry," Gideon yelled.

Tom and George came running upstairs. "And now someone's taking shots at you?" his father bellowed.

"No. I don't think so. I think they shot out the light and made a very good, non-lethal shot on a person standing 10 feet from me. I think they hit exactly where they intended," Gideon presumed. His eyes grew large, and he scrambled to his feet, running for the front door. "Tracey!" he yelled as George tackled him.

"No, you don't," George hollered. "You do not step foot back outside until it's been cleared. Trent will take care of Tracey."

Cal went pale and started to shake. "Gigi," he muttered. He grabbed Tom's sleeve. "Gigi's pregnant."

———

Tracey, in her underwear, opened the garment bag and pulled out the delicate lacy veil attached to a buckwheat flower laurel. She slipped it onto her head and reached back into the bag, pulling out a white silk slip dress embroidered with beaded buckwheat flowers all over. "Oh, that's lovely," Gigi said.

Tracey slipped it on, and Gigi zipped it up the back.

"Wow," she said. "I'm hot."

Gigi laughed. "Yeah, you are."

The dress hugged her body in all the right places. "There's more," Tracey observed, pulling out a chima, a floor-length pleated skirt that started at the chest and cascaded in fountains of white silk to the floor, and a jeogori, a short jacket that fell just below the chest, with long full sleeves that fell nearly to the hem of the skirt. The jeogori was, like the slip dress, intricately embroidered with beaded white buckwheat flowers. "Oh...it's a traditional hanbok," Tracey exclaimed, tears coming to her eyes. "It's so beautiful."

"It is pretty," Gigi agreed. She helped Tracey pull on the tulle slip over the slip dress, and then, between the two of them, they figured out how to put on the hanbok. "So, the slip dress is for the reception after. Awesome."

Tracey walked out to the living room to the "oohs" and "ahs" from her aunt, mother-in-law, and sister-in-law. She did a spin in the middle of the floor as Trent's phone rang. He silently answered the call, stood abruptly, and pulled his weapon. "Close the blinds, Mrs. Davison," he said to Hana Jin, who was closest to the window.

She did as he said, and he flipped off the lights. "The dining room is an interior room. Ladies, please go into the dining room. Do not turn on the lights," he said, taking position by the door.

"What happened?" implored a panicked Tracey, as Hana Jin pulled her into the dining room.

Tracey sat, worried, at the dining room table. Gigi reached for a margarita. Tracey smacked her hand. "That's Janey's," she said, biting her lip.

"Oh, I don't mind," Janey offered. "I think we could all

use a sip." She was the only one who'd brought her drink into the dining room with them.

"She can't have alcohol," Tracey announced.

Gigi's back stiffened, and her hand went instinctively to her belly. "Does it show?" she whispered.

"No, but you never turn down a margarita, and tonight you were drinking virgins. I can add 2 plus 2," Tracey replied, as the night outside filled with sirens.

Tracey's phone beeped from the coffee table. Trent cautiously made his way over and picked it up. "Passcode, Trace?" he called.

"6422," Tracey called back.

"Huh," he said, looking at the phone. "That should keep you from walking down the aisle. His best man has a bullet in his leg." He looked up at Tracey from across the room. "From Christine Richards."

"Isaac!" Janey sobbed.

CHAPTER 15

"Yes, sir. She received a text from a number identified as 'Christine Richards.' Yes. It indicates that Isaac was the intended victim to prevent the wedding from occurring. The children are upstairs playing. Everybody is safe. Okay. Will do," Trent said into his phone. He disconnected and turned to the ladies. "The situation is controlled. The shooter is still at large, but Officers Benson and Phillips are on their way. They can take Janey and Nettie Spencer to the hospital. Isaac has been transported there. The rest should shelter in place, but it is believed the danger has passed. They found the weapon abandoned in the woods."

The door burst open as he spoke. Gideon and Cal rushed inside. "Tracey!" Gideon yelled.

She jumped up and ran to him. Crying, she threw herself into his arms. "You're okay? You're alright?" he asked, holding her at arm's length to look at her. "Oh, wow. You're beautiful," he sputtered.

She blushed. "You aren't supposed to see," she said, stepping back.

"You're beautiful," he repeated, pulling her close again and wrapping her in his embrace.

Cal sought out Gigi and rushed to her. "Gigi?" he said, stopping short as she stood. He seemed to need to catch his breath. "Are you okay?"

"I'm fine," she said, staring at him.

"Oh. Thank God," he proclaimed, taking two steps

toward her, before she rushed at him, collapsing against him in tears.

"I was so scared!" she wailed.

"Me too. Me too," he cried.

"Let me see the damn phone," Gideon snapped, holding out his hand to Trent, who handed him Tracey's phone cautiously.

He pulled up the text. Tracey looked over his shoulder. "It's Christine's number. And that shot...that shot wasn't pulled off by Lisa Biacchi." He frowned. "Damn it. Lena."

"Christine's mother?" Tracey asked, surprised. She had seemed so nice.

"Siri, look up Lena Vuković," he said into the phone.

"Lena Vuković was a Bosnian Serbian sniper during the Croatian War of Independence," Siri answered.

Tracey's mouth dropped open. "Lena Richards was a sniper?"

Gideon slowly nodded.

"And she has Christine's old phone," Tracey realized.

"I never liked that bitch," Nettie proclaimed.

Tracey grabbed Gigi by the arm and pulled her into the bedroom. "Help me out of this," she implored. They removed the wedding dress carefully, but quickly, replacing it in the garment bag. Tracey threw on one of Gideon's sweaters, because it was lying on the dresser, and a pair of jeans.

Tracey stepped into a pair of sneakers. She practically ran back into the living room. "Cassie!" she called. Janey was already putting Sam's coat on him, and Nettie was zipping Vivi's. "Come on. We're going with Daddy!" Cassie bounded down the steps. Tracey took her coat off the hook by the door and held it out to her.

"Tracey!" Gideon reprimanded. "You two should stay here."

She stood up straight, looking him right in the eyes. "We're going with you."

He looked like he was about to argue. But his mother said, "Oh, good. Tracey, be sure he doesn't drive like a maniac. I've just talked to Tom, and Isaac is going to be fine. Gideon needs to calm down and remember you and Cassie are in the car with him."

He closed his mouth and took Cassie's coat from Tracey, kneeling to help Cassie put it on. Tracey put on her own coat.

Gigi put her arm around Cal's waist. "We'll just stay here, if that's okay," she said. "We need to talk."

"Of course," Tracey said, opening the door. "We'll be back as soon as we can. Love you, Geeg."

"Love you, too, Trace," Gigi replied.

With that, everybody except Gigi and Cal headed out. Hana Jin got a ride with Nettie and Janey. Gideon put Cassie in her booster in the back seat of the truck. Trent climbed into the backseat as well. Tracey got in the passenger seat, and Gideon drove.

"Mistwer Twent," Cassie said as they pulled out of the driveway, "Are you Mommy or Daddy's bes fend? Cuz Gigi says she's Mommy's."

"I'm both their friend," he said coolly. "You can have more than one best friend, Sweetheart, and you can be more than one person's friend."

————*

It was bedlam in the emergency room. George was already there. Tom had gone back with Isaac. Hana Jin ran to George and hugged him, yelling "Yeobo, yeobo!" as she walked through the door.

"What's that?" Nettie whispered to Tracey.

"It's 'Darling' or 'Honey,'" Tracey whispered back, shifting Cassie on her hip.

"'Ya bow' is honey? I like honey. Granny gives me honey in my tea when I have a sore throat," Cassie said loudly.

"Not that kind of honey. 'Honey,' like I call your daddy," Tracey explained.

Nettie and Janey both wanted to see Isaac, but the nurse wasn't letting them back, since Tom was already with him. Gideon was trying to explain to George his theory about Lena Richards. Trent was trying to keep himself between Tracey and the door, but she kept moving. The sheriff had arrived and was trying to get statements. Plus, there were three patients waiting to be taken back, and their families.

The poor nurse looked overwhelmed.

Tracey grabbed Gideon's hand. "Come on, Baby. Let's get some coffee. We're not helping in here," she said.

He nodded and put his arm around her waist. "You may be right," he agreed. Her heart raced. He was so sexy. She still couldn't believe a guy like him loved her.

She took Cassie's hand, and Gideon wrapped his arm around her waist as they walked toward the cafeteria. She felt safe and cherished. She took a seat at a table in the corner while Gideon bought two coffees and a chocolate milk.

He sat across from her, handing her a coffee.

"Are you okay?" he asked, worry etched on his face. There was a slight tremor in his voice.

Tracey nodded. "Trent was there. I was perfectly safe. Cassie was safe," she answered. She swallowed hard. "You could have been killed." Her eyes filled with tears.

"I wasn't...she wasn't trying to kill me. Isaac...He lost a lot of blood," Gideon explained.

"Is Uncle Isaac going to be okay, Daddy?" Cassie asked, suddenly upset.

He nodded and held out his arms to her. She climbed onto his lap, and he hugged her tightly. "He'll be fine, Baby."

They sat and drank their coffees. After about 20 minutes, Sheriff Townsend entered the cafeteria. He nodded at Gideon as he ordered a coffee. Once he paid, he walked over to the table where Gideon and Tracey sat.

"You were right. Gary and Lena Richards were stopped by state police on Route 7 heading south, 5 miles north of Dexter. Apparently, Lena has been...committed since Christine disappeared 4 years ago. Gary figured out what she did and was trying to get her out of Maine and back to the hospital in New York. She had Christine's phone in her purse."

"So, it's over?" Tracey asked, taking Gideon's hand.

He sighed. "Well, that threat is," he said, smiling weakly.

She nodded. Of course. There was still the question of Lisa Biacchi and the missing women...and Dom was still missing.

"I say we just announce that we're already married," she suggested. "I hate all this secrecy."

"Okay," Gideon answered. "Whatever you want, Babe. I'll do it."

"Already...married? Um...congratulations," the sheriff stammered.

"Thanks, Ralph," Gideon said. His voice was weary. Worry was still etched on his face.

CHAPTER 16

It was a sleepless night. George took Tracey and Cassie back to Goose Fields Farm after Isaac was out of surgery around 11 pm. Gideon wanted to stay with his brother and was confident Trent would keep his wife and child safe.

Janey's parents came to get Vivi and Sam. Isaac was sleeping soundly. Gideon and Isaac's parents had fallen asleep in the chairs in Isaac's room. Janey looked at Gideon. It was close to 3 am. He swallowed hard. "I'm so sorry, Janey," he sniffed.

"For what? Saving him?"

"I'm sorry that...he was hurt because of me."

"Don't be ridiculous, Gideon," Janey scolded him. "You cannot be held accountable for someone else's psychosis."

"You tell him, Babe," Isaac groaned, awakening.

"Hey," Gideon gasped, grabbing his brother's hand. "You're awake."

"Hmmm. I feel like hell," Isaac said.

Janey leaned down and kissed his forehead. "You scared the crap out of us," she sobbed.

"Sorry," he croaked. "Did you catch them?" He squeezed Gideon's hand.

Gideon sniffed. "Ayuh. It was Lena...Christine's mom. She was a sniper in Croatia back in her youth. The state police picked her and Gary up just outside Dexter."

Isaac groaned as he shifted in the bed. "Was she trying to hit you?"

"No. She was aiming for you. She texted Tracey that your injury should stop us from getting married," Gideon replied, unable to look Isaac in the eyes.

"That's just demented," Isaac said with a slight laugh. "Hey…Gid…you know this isn't your fault? If you want to blame anything, aside from the warped mind of Lena Richards, blame Marty Moose for drawing us outside."

"I know. Cognitively, I know. Still feels like my fault," Gideon said, biting his lip.

"Yeah, well, get over it," Isaac chided him. "Tracey okay?"

"Tracey's fine," Gideon laughed.

———

At 4:30, Tracey gave up on trying to sleep. She climbed out of the bed, dressed in jeans and a sweatshirt, and slipped on her neck brace. She ran a brush through her hair and stared at her reflection in the bathroom mirror.

"Mama," she said out loud. "I know you were battling some demons, but at least you were only your own worst enemy. How could she do this? How could anybody?" She felt the sting in her eyes as she fought the tears. Her throat tightened. She hugged herself and gave in. Sobs wracked her body, and she sank to the floor.

She didn't know how long she lay on the floor crying, but suddenly his strong arms were lifting her. Gideon silently picked her up and carried her back to the bed. He sat on the edge of the bed, with her wrapped up in his arms on his lap. He held her close. She clung to him, not ever wanting to let go. She cried into his chest while he held her.

She snuggled in against him, nuzzling his neck under his jawline. She sniffed and wrapped her arms around his neck. She trailed kisses up his neck to his mouth. He pulled her close and kissed her deeply, removing the neck brace and laying her on the bed. She wrapped herself around him as he lowered himself on top of her. "I love you, Gideon," she whispered. "I don't want to lose you."

"You won't. I won't let that happen," Gideon whispered in her ear before sucking her earlobe into his mouth.

———

Gigi took Cal's hand. "I was wrong," she said, looking at the sunrise and not at him as they stood on the front porch together.

"About what, Honey?" he asked, kissing the hand in his.

"I love you," she replied.

"You were wrong about loving me?" he chuckled.

"No. You goof. I was wrong about *not* loving you," she sniffed.

He laughed. "Ahhhh. I see. You thought you didn't love me, but you really do."

"Stop it, Cal. I'm being serious. I had it all wrong. I thought love was something entirely different. I didn't understand until someone was shooting a gun in your direction that I...couldn't live without you."

"That's alright, Sweetheart. I knew you couldn't."

"You did? Why didn't you tell me?" she asked, turning to look at him. Her expression was so earnest, he had to laugh.

"You had to figure it out for yourself, Geege. Sorry," he replied with a coy smile.

"How do you feel about me?" she asked nervously.

"Like you are the sun and the moon," he said, winking.

"Calvin Johnson!" she exclaimed incredulously.

"Gigi, you are my entire world. You and the baby. You're all I think about. You're all I want. Does that answer your question?" Cal said earnestly.

She flung herself into his arms and hugged him tightly. "Can I say yes now? Or do I have to wait for you to ask me again?"

"Well, can I ask again now?" he suggested.

She took a step backwards. "Cal? Are you..."

He dropped to one knee and pulled the ring box out of his hoodie pocket.

———

As Gideon drifted off to sleep, Gigi's squeal pierced the silence. Both Tracey and Gideon sat bolt upright. "Ow," she said, grabbing her neck.

"You okay?" Gideon asked. "What the heck was that?"

Gigi burst into the room and jumped into the bed between them. Gideon grabbed blankets up over himself and rolled away, falling off the side of the bed to the floor, taking the duvet with him. Tracey, likewise, pulled covers over herself. Meanwhile, Gigi screamed unintelligible sounds. Tracey squealed in response, and the two women locked hands and began bouncing on the bed. Gideon stared, unable to comprehend anything his wife and her best friend were saying. Then Tracey took Gigi's left hand and gazed at the ring on her finger.

"Jesus, you scared the crap out of me," he said. He looked up to see Cal standing in the doorway with his mouth open. "I'm so sorry," he said to Gideon, sitting unceremoniously on the floor.

"No problem," Gideon laughed. "Congratulations."

———

After Gideon showered, the four of them sat around the kitchen table. Tracey threw her arm around Gigi's shoulder as they sat side by side. "I'm so happy for you, Gigi."

"That's what I should have said to you, Tracey. I'm sorry," Gigi replied, laying her head on Tracey's shoulder and holding her hand out in front of her face to admire the ring again.

"That goes for both of us," Cal added. "I think we were so wrapped up in how quick it was that we neglected to account for love."

Gideon smiled. "We know it seems fast to the world, but I promise it's not to us."

Tracey nodded. "It's been a decade, Geege."

Gigi looked at her. "The dream thing? You both believe this?"

Gideon sighed. "I know it. I've met her in my dreams. I know everything about her. She knows everything about me."

"I don't see how that's possible," Cal added.

"I can't explain it. I just know it's true," Tracey said.

Cal grinned. "Did you have sex?"

Tracey blushed.

"You did!" Gigi teased. "Okay, so how did the dream compare to the reality?"

"Reality is better," Tracey groaned. "I mean, it's a dream. You don't actually...feel or smell. It's more sound and sight. But it was all...very accurate."

It was Gideon's turn to blush. "Jesus, Tracey," he groaned, burying his head in his hand.

"Well, it was," she insisted.

"Yes, but it's nobody's business," he replied.

"That's in retrospect," Gigi said. "You added details in your mind after the fact."

Gideon sighed again. "Tracey's tattoo above her hip… the lotus flower…" he started.

Gigi smiled warily. "Yeah?"

"It covers a scar…a crescent-shaped scar."

The smile vanished from Gigi's face. "Did she tell you?"

"I've never told anyone," Tracey assured her. "Not even in my dreams."

"You did."

"When?" she demanded.

"The night it happened," Gideon said, sniffing. "It… was my 13th birthday and the first time I met you on the shore of Lake Sebec."

Tracey furrowed her brow. "Deon?"

"Gideon," he replied. They stared at each other. "You went to that party with Gigi. Tiffany Martin invited you as a joke…to make fun of you. She said that boy, Malcolm Jenkins, liked Gigi. But it was all a setup, and Tiffany and her friends laughed at you. Tracey shoved her into the pool…and the two of you were walking away to leave. That Malcolm guy grabbed Gigi and said he'd be okay if she put out. He ripped her shirt. Tracey got between him and Gigi. He shoved her into a trash bag…and there was a broken bottle in the bag. She fell on it."

"The fever," Tracey whispered. "I did dream of a lake… and a boy. He said it was his birthday. But that it had been a bad birthday. His grandmother died the week before, and everybody was sad. His parents said, "Happy Birthday," but they didn't feel up to celebrating. Then he got food poisoning and was stuck in the hospital. I told him I was sick, too. I told him I wished I had a cake, and a cake appeared. We sat and ate cake...and...that...was real? That was you?"

"I...knew you the second I saw you at MIT, Tracey. Those...eyes."

"So, you both dreamed you ate cake?" Gigi scoffed.

"It was more than that," Tracey said, blushing.

"What? Did you kiss?" Gigi teased.

Tracey blushed harder.

"It was the first time I ever dreamed about kissing," Gideon admitted.

Cal smiled. "You just had similar dreams, is all."

Gideon was quiet. Finally, he stood. "Come with me," he said, walking toward the door. They followed.

Trent, outside on the porch, fell in step behind them as they trudged down the lane toward the burned-out trailer. Gideon continued past the trailer and the Christmas Tree farm. He rounded a corner and approached his parents' house. He pointed at a bush at the end of the driveway. "Wait here," he said, continuing on his way around the back of the house.

The group huddled uncomfortably by the bush.

He returned moments later with a shovel.

"What on earth are you doing?" Tracey asked as he stabbed the shovel into the ground, digging up the bush.

He didn't answer. He worked until he had the bush completely dug up and a hole where the bush had been. He looked into the hole and smiled. "Gigi, come get this time capsule, please. I don't want to touch it. I want to maintain the integrity of the time capsule," he said.

Gigi looked puzzled, but she walked over to the hole, squatted down, brushed some dirt away, and pulled a metal box out of the hole.

"You dug up a time capsule?" Tracey asked, perplexed.

He smiled at her and pointed to the friendship bracelet on her wrist. "That isn't the original."

The hair stood up on the back of her neck as she stepped forward and knelt on the ground beside Gigi. Gigi laughed and opened the box. Inside were the normal boyhood things: baseball cards, a Spiderman comic, a baseball, a dog's collar… and a friendship bracelet.

Tracey gasped and picked up the bracelet, turning it over to see written in Sharpie in Gigi's big print, "G.W. and T.H. Friends 4ever." The dot over the "i" was a heart.

"It's the friendship bracelet I lost at MCV," she confirmed. "How?"

"I found it in my hospital room at Mayo when I woke up," Gideon said.

"How is that even possible?" she asked him.

"Tracey, I don't even know how it's possible to share one dream, let alone years of dreams. There is no way I can explain any of this. But even then, I knew this belonged to you. I don't know how I ended up with it."

CHAPTER 17

Tracey and Gigi knocked on the door to Isaac and Janey's house. Sam opened the door and aimed a toy gun at them before lowering it and saying, "Oh, it's just Aunt Tracey and her friend," before skulking off. Janey, flustered, appeared at the door.

"Hey, Tracey...Gigi. Come on in," she said, opening the door to them.

"Isaac home?" Tracey asked, stepping across the threshold and handing Janey a bag full of uneaten tacos from the night before.

"Hmmm. Ayuh, about an hour ago. He's a bear, though," she replied. "Isaac!" she called, "Tracey's here ta see yuh." She motioned down the hallway. "He's in the family room, laid out on the couch."

Tracey smiled and nodded. "How is he? Aside from a bit grumpy?" she whispered.

"He's okay, praise God," Janey whispered back. "I know he's in some pain, but he's holding up."

"Isaac!" Tracey called. "You want some tacos?"

"Of course I want tacos. What kind of question is that?" Isaac bellowed from down the hallway. Janey rolled her eyes and shook her head.

Tracey grinned and walked toward the sound of her brother-in-law's voice. Gigi followed, and Janey closed the door.

Isaac, with his leg propped up, lay perched on a giant

red leather sofa with a remote control pointed at a giant TV on the wall opposite him. He had paused his channel surfing on a trout fishing show.

"Hey there, Isaac," Tracey greeted him. "How are you feeling?"

"Like pure shit, Tracey," he grumbled. He looked past Tracey at Gigi. "You and the little one ok, Miss Winston? Cal surely was worried."

Gigi blushed adorably. "We were all fine. Thank you for asking."

He nodded. "I like that Cal. He's pretty useless around the sheep, but he's a good guy."

Tracey set the bag of tacos on the coffee table. "I'm so sorry you were hurt, Isaac," she offered.

"Oh, it's not your fault," he said, shifting and grimacing. "Not like you could have prevented it."

Tracey took two steps back. "Gideon and I got married a few days ago," she blurted before turning and running out of the room.

"You what?" he yelled at her retreating form. He grabbed a pillow from behind him and flung it at her. It bounced off the door jamb and fell to the floor.

————

Gideon hadn't slept much and was concerned about his brother, but the sheriff's office was down a deputy. He forced himself to don his uniform and drive into town. He fell into his desk chair and lay his head on the wooden desktop, closing his eyes.

"Gideon," Brenda said softly. "You have a call."

He opened his eyes and sat up. "Ayuh, put it through," he replied huskily.

The shrill ring of the phone on his desk pierced the quiet of the office. He picked it up. "Deputy Spencer," he said into the receiver.

"Hey there, Spencer. It's been a while," the familiar voice chirped.

"Scott," Gideon breathed in relief. "Thanks for calling me back."

Scott Unger had been Gideon's roommate at MIT. He was also a trust fund kid and was currently employed at his family's foundation. The Unger Foundation awarded scholarships to undergraduates in STEM programs throughout the US. They also funded research in the sciences...any science.

"You bet, Buddy. What's up?" Scott queried.

"Do you remember Lisa Biacchi? The girl who got hazed?" he asked.

"Biacchi? Um...I think so. Biacchi...Biacchi...An Unger Scholarship recipient. From Trenton."

"Trenton? New Jersey?" Gideon said, his brow furrowing. His eyes narrowed, and his jaw tightened.

"Um...yes," Scott replied after Gideon heard his tapping on his keyboard. "Why?"

"I...she's a person of interest, is all I can say," Gideon answered. "Anything a matter of public record?"

"Oh, sure. Her essay and biography are published on our foundation's website. I'll send you the link. What's your cell?"

Gideon gave his friend his number. He opened the link. There she was. Lisa Biacchi... as he remembered her from his senior year at MIT, 50 pounds thinner, 6 years younger.

Her biography indicated that she was a graduate

of Trenton Central High School, the only child of Charlise Biacchi, a waitress. She did not know her father as he had died when she was young. She had a half-brother, a Navy man, with whom she shared a close relationship. She excelled in science and wanted to be an aerospace engineer. Her dream was to work on a Mars expedition.

Gideon shut his eyes and breathed out a raspy breath. He hated what he was thinking, but how could he not? Dom was from Trenton. Dom had been in the Navy. Dom's father had died when he was young. He had never mentioned a half-sister, but why would he if he was helping her? If he were helping her, he wouldn't. Then he had a truly horrible thought. What if it were the other way round, and she was helping him? He picked up the receiver on the desk phone and dialed the sheriff's extension. "You have to see this," he said when Ralph answered.

CHAPTER 18

George looked at Hannah. She was still beautiful, still a free spirit. Hyun Hana Jin was a starving artist when George's partner, Seong Min, had introduced him to his sister. She dabbled in sculpture, but painting was her passion.

"This is my sister, Hana Jin," Seong Min had said, motioning to the most beautiful woman George had ever seen. She had green and red paint smeared on her cheek, appropriate for the season. It had been two days before Christmas.

"Hannah?" George had repeated, reaching out to shake her hand. She placed her delicate hand in his.

"It is now," she had said, smiling up at him from the stool she was perched on in front of her easel.

"What is?" he had asked, completely befuddled and bewitched.

"My name," she had replied.

Meanwhile, he had been holding her hand. Seong had laughed. "You gonna keep that forever, George?" he had asked, nodding at their hands.

"Yes," George had answered, smiling.

He had meant it. He reached out and took his wife's hand now...thirty years later...as she mindlessly flipped through the bridal magazine. She was sitting on the hotel room bed. Her back against the headboard, her legs stretched out in front of her and crossed at the ankles. She looked elegant. There was no other word for it.

She smiled as he entwined his fingers with hers. Her smile was warm and stretched all the way into her beautiful black eyes. Those deep, dark pools strangely lit up with her smile. The curve of her mouth gently bowed up. Her lips looked delicious.

"Why are you staring at me, George?" she teased.

"Because that's what people do, Hannah. They stare at beauty," he whispered in her ear.

She laughed and set aside the magazine. "You're such a romantic sap," she cooed as he kissed her.

The banging on the door interrupted them, and George swore softly under his breath.

"George!" Gideon's voice called from outside the door.

George sighed heavily and rose, crossing the hotel room in 5 easy strides to the door. He yanked the door open aggressively and stood looking at the young deputy for a moment. Gideon was positively disheveled. His hair was mussed, and his uniform shirt was slightly wrinkled, like he'd fallen asleep with it on, which he probably had, given how little sleep he would have gotten the night before.

"What is it?" George prompted.

"Oh. I'm sorry to interrupt…but… Dominic Moretti is Lisa Biacchi's half-brother." The deputy shoved a tablet at George.

George looked down at the information Gideon had gathered and swore again. This time, out loud. "Shit," he exclaimed. He turned and smiled sadly at his wife. "I'm sorry, Sweetheart, I have to go back to work."

She nodded and picked back up the bridal magazine, waving him off.

Nettie Spencer pushed open the door to the large, unused greenhouse. She could see it all...exactly what she wanted from the glass building. Tom had basically cleaned it out last year when she had first presented the idea of opening a wedding planning business with Janey and using the old greenhouse as a wedding venue. It was empty now.

She grabbed the broom she'd brought out here with her firmly by the handle and went to work sweeping the concrete floor. The work settled her nerves and focused her energy on something other than worrying about her sons.

Gideon was rushing into marriage. No matter how much she liked Tracey...and she did...very much, this was incredibly fast. She wondered when he'd brought Tracey by that first morning if he was anxious about providing a mother for Cassie. After all, that was the morning they found Christine. Then again, he genuinely seemed to be in love with Tracey. And she seemed to love him. Nettie just couldn't understand the rush to the altar.

And now, Isaac had been shot in the leg. He wasn't the kind of man to sit around when there was work to be done. Janey was never going to be able to keep him from aggravating his wound.

Her heart simply ached.

So, she focused on sweeping the floor of the greenhouse.

She focused so intensely that she never heard Tom approach. She looked up, and there he was with Hannah Davison, Tracey's aunt.

Her husband frowned, took the broom from her, and hugged her. "It will all be alright, Nettie, my darling. They're grown men," he said in a soothing voice. He knew her so well.

"Are you worried about Tracey and Gideon getting married?" Hannah asked, taking the broom from Tom. "I admit I was, too. George was just pleased that Gideon is such an upstanding young man," she admitted.

Nettie laughed. "He is an upstanding young man," she concurred. "And I adore Tracey. I do. I...it's just so fast."

Hannah stepped closer. "There's nothing we can do. They're already married," she announced. "George stood with Gideon."

————

Gideon drove as George read Dom's background check. "It doesn't mention a sister," George noted.

"Half-sister," Gideon corrected. "It wouldn't. But it seemed like too much of a coincidence that Lisa Biacchi's half-brother would have been in the Navy, and they were both from Trenton. They went to the same high school. So, I pulled Dom's birth certificate. His father was listed as Mario Moretti. Lisa's father is also listed as Mario Moretti on her birth certificate. The address given for Mr. Moretti on both birth certificates was 112 Trenton Ave. Lisa was given her mother's last name."

Gideon turned into the parking lot of the apartment building where Dom lived and found a parking space. The sheriff had already searched Dom's apartment after his disappearance, but he hadn't known about Dom's relationship to the alleged perpetrator. Gideon didn't expect to find much, but maybe there was a clue as to where they might be. It was a long shot, he knew.

George followed him into the apartment. Gideon had been here on a few occasions to play poker. He didn't need to search for the light switch. He flipped on the lights and looked in the bowl below the switch on a table by the door. Dom's extra keys were in the bowl, along with some mail. Gideon picked up the stack of mail and flipped through it. As expected, there was nothing incriminating there, just Dom's electric bill, a catalog from Bass Pro-Shop, and a bank statement. He picked up the keys. The apartment key was on the ring, along with a key to Dom's truck. There was also a safe deposit box key. Gideon held it up. George nodded.

Gideon bagged the keyring before they moved deeper into the apartment.

As he searched through Dom's desk, his cell phone rang. He pulled it out of his pocket. Dom's number appeared on the screen. Gideon looked up and found the camera hidden in the plant on the top of the roll-top desk. He grimaced at the plant and answered the call.

"Dom?" he said.

George froze and stood straight.

"Hey, Gideon," Dom said. "Put me on speaker."

Gideon did as Dom requested.

"I guess you know," the deputy's voice extolled sadly over the call. "Lisa has been obsessed with you ever since you saved her. I honestly only applied to the sheriff's department to check you out…do a little investigating about where you came from. I never expected you to come to work at the sheriff's office after Christine…let's say 'disappeared.'"

"What the hell, man?" Gideon questioned. "We were friends. At least I thought we were."

"We are friends," Dom replied. He laughed. Gideon stared at the camera in the plant.

"Great. Then tell me where the missing women are and bring yourself and Lisa in," Gideon said, smiling coyly.

"I don't think so," Dom said as he hung up.

CHAPTER 19

As the sun set, Tracey's phone chirped at her. Gideon had texted.

"I'll be home late, Baby," the text read. "Don't wait up."

She sighed and swallowed the last sip of her glass of wine. Cassie was already in bed. Gigi and Cal were in their own little world, curled up together on the sofa in front of the fire, while Tracey washed the dishes, alone in the kitchen.

She texted back, "Okay. I miss you. I love you."

The phone chirped again. "I love you, too, Tracey. More than anything."

She grabbed the wine bottle off the counter and poured herself another glass of Merlot.

Earlier, Nettie had descended upon the house in a cascade of tears. Aunt Hannah had told her that Tracey and Gideon were already married. Her mother-in-law, like everyone else, was already fearful that Tracey and Gideon were rushing into marriage. She had reluctantly agreed to help plan the hasty wedding, perhaps in hopes of talking the young couple into postponing it. To learn that they hadn't even waited for the wedding to get married had been devastating to Nettie.

Aunt Hannah, who had arrived with Nettie, had stated that she understood, though her free spirit was far more accepting. She confessed that she had married George after knowing him for only a month. By comparison, the two and a half months that Gideon and Tracey had known and lived together seemed like a long time.

Gigi had soothed Nettie. She told Gideon's mother that she had doubts when she arrived, but that she now believed Tracey and Gideon were prepared and knew what they were doing. What's more, they truly loved each other. She didn't explain why she had changed her mind. Gigi had professed that no one would believe it. Tracey knew that was true. She'd had a hard time believing it herself, and she had experienced it.

Cassie had ultimately been the catalyst for peace. She had run downstairs and jumped into Nettie's loving arms, excited about the dress she was going to wear and full of questions about the wedding.

"Aren't you afraid that things are changing so fast?" Nettie asked the little girl.

"Nothing's changing," Cassie replied. "Tracey's already my mommy. We're just getting married to make it legal."

"But why do we need to have a wedding then?" Nettie asked.

"We don't need to," Cassie said after a moment's thought. "We want to because we want to have fun with all our family and friends, because we are a family."

The fact that Cassie already saw Tracey as her mother and the wedding as a celebration of what already was, not as a change in her life, seemed to have eased Nettie's mind again.

The phone rang once more, and Tracey looked at the caller ID. "Hello, Nettie," she said into it, trying to sound cheerful.

"I'm sorry, Tracey. I shouldn't have unloaded on you this afternoon," her mother-in-law exclaimed. "You're both adults. I hope you don't hold my outburst against me."

"I know you're worried about Gideon, Nettie. I think it's perfectly natural. But I swear, I really do love him. I...I've never had a family...at least not that I remember clearly. My mother told me that her parents had died before I was born and that my father died when I was a baby. She lied. And I'm angry about that, but I also understand she had crushing depression and mental illness. I honestly feel blessed that I have found Gideon and Cassie...and by extension all of you. I feel like I have a family for the first time in my life. I'd never hold your concerns against you. I love you. I hope you'll come to love me, too."

Nettie was silent as she spoke. When she finished, Nettie replied, "Of course, I love you. You are a part of this family. I was just...I don't know."

"You were hurt. We got married, and we didn't include you. It was a spur of the moment decision, and we were wrong. I'm sorry. We should have considered your feelings. And we didn't." Tracey apologized.

"Thank you, Sweetheart," Nettie said, crying. "Thanks for understanding."

———

Gideon slept as George drove south toward Boston. The lights of the oncoming traffic fell on the younger man's sleeping form. George didn't blame him. He'd not slept for close to 48 hours now...well, any real sleep.

He was a good kid. George prided himself on being a good judge of character. Gideon had a good one. He was smart, hardworking, and honest. He'd liked him instantly.

Dom…not so much. He hadn't pegged him as a suspect, but he'd certainly disliked the man. He reached for the radio dial and changed the station, finding a soft rock station.

After they had learned that Dom and Lisa Biacchi were half-siblings, they had searched Dom's apartment again. It would have proved a fruitless effort had Gideon not seen the hidden internet camera in a plant. It prompted Dom to call Gideon. When Gideon pulled the camera out, he found a label on it that read "Biacchi Systems, Inc.," with a Boston address. The business did not appear to be registered. And the address was a residence…in fact, a home in Beacon Hill belonging to the Kingsford family. A further search of the safety deposit box for which they had found the key at Dom's apartment produced a stash of photos of Dom and Lisa, many in Piscataquis County, and photos of Gideon, taken with a long-distance lens, taken over the last several years.

A call to Phillip Kingsford, IV, prompted an invitation by the CEO of Kingsford Technologies for George and Gideon to meet him at The 'Quin House for a late dinner at 9 pm. When they left Dover-Foxcroft, they had 4 hours to get there, and that would be about what they'd need.

The kid had fallen asleep almost as soon as they had left the little town behind them.

George was struck by how similar to Seong Min Gideon was. He thought back to when he'd first met Tracey's father, 31 years ago. "Shawn" Hyun was freshly promoted to detective. George was his first partner. Gideon, naturally, didn't look like Shawn. Shawn was, after all, Korean, and Gideon was Caucasian. But they had similar educational backgrounds: MIT, followed by Boston College. He'd scoffed at first when he learned about Shawn's education, but his partner quickly showed that he was more than just book smart. Shawn and Judith were dating when George was first assigned to work with him.

It had been about six months when Shawn asked George to be his best man. And by God, that man loved Judith with his whole being. George had been honored to stand with him. He could see Gideon looking at Tracey the same way Shawn had looked at Judith.

Even before he'd learned who Tracey was, he'd thought Gideon was like his late partner. Right from the start, he'd seen that same spark for the job in the young deputy that he'd seen in Tracey's father, the same drive, the same values.

That first night after meeting Gideon and finding Tracey at long last, Shawn had come to him in a dream. It had felt so real. He opened the hotel room door at the Lodge, and there stood Shawn, in uniform, just like the day he'd met him.

Shawn had looked up from the ground when the door opened, had smiled, and had said, "Hey, Georgie. Long time no see."

It had been so real, George had to look around to check his surroundings, and when he looked back at the bed, he saw his own self soundly sleeping in the bed. Confused and disoriented, he'd turned back to Shawn. "Wha...What?" he'd stammered.

"You're dreaming," Shawn had replied with a sly grin. "You found her! I knew you would."

"I...Yes, by sheer chance. I looked, but Judith eluded me at every turn. She'd move every time I located her...until...I gave up. I'm so sorry," George had pled to the apparition.

Shawn's hand on his shoulder felt real enough, though.

"No worries. What do you think of him?" Shawn had

asked.

"I...I like him," George had replied.

"Hmmm. Me too. I always did."

As he drove now, he looked at the sleeping deputy who shifted his weight in the passenger's seat of the Tahoe, and he wondered what that meant. How could Shawn have always liked someone whom he'd never met? Gideon was only 29 years old. He would have been seven when Shawn was killed. It was true that Gideon grew up on the neighboring farm to Judith's parents, but she had long been estranged from her parents by that time. Shawn had never met her parents, had never been to Piscataquis County. Judith had sworn she'd never return to Goose Fields Farm.

Gideon snorted in his sleep and startled awake, saying, "Don't!" as he sat up straight.

"Don't what?" George chuckled.

Gideon looked around the cab of the SUV, dazed for a second, shook his head, and answered, "Oh, sorry. I drifted off there for a minute. Where are we?"

George laughed. "Ayuh, just for a minute. We're just outside Boston."

"I slept 3 and a half hours?" Gideon asked.

"Ayuh," George chuckled.

———

Gideon slipped on the dinner jacket and the tie the attendant handed him. "Well, this looks stupid," he grumbled, straightening the tie. George had his own in the Tahoe, so his jacket at least fit him, whereas Gideon's was at least two sizes too large. "I might as well have a neon sign over my head that blinks, 'Does Not Belong Here!'"

George chuckled again. "Wanna switch?"

Gideon shook his head and laughed. "Nah, sir. I can withstand the scrutiny." He liked George. Most guys would just say, 'better you than me,' and leave it at that. George wasn't that kind. He was almost as old as Gideon's father, but he had a youthful quality about him.

The two of them were led to a table in the VIP section of the club. Phillip Kingsford IV had not arrived yet, but had advised the club that they would be joining him for dinner. The Maître D' handed them their menus and snapped his fingers as they sat. A server immediately appeared.

"Mr. Kingsford asked that you go ahead and order before he arrives. Anything on the menu, Gentlemen. It's on his tab."

Gideon raised an eyebrow. The menu only listed the items, no prices. He was starved, having missed lunch...and dinner. "That's...generous," he stated.

"Go hog wild," George said, winking.

"I'd love a ribeye, medium rare," he said, perusing the items.

"Yes, sir," the waiter said, nodding.

They placed their drink and dinner orders. Gideon shifted uncomfortably in his seat. "I hate this place," he mumbled.

"You've been here before?" George inquired, taking a drink of his water.

"Mmmm. Ayuh. With Scott Unger. He was my roommate at MIT," Gideon replied.

"Oh, James Unger's son?"

"You know Mr. Unger?" Gideon asked, smiling.

"Not personally, no. Shawn...Seong Min...knew him. I believe they were roommates at MIT," George told him.

"Huh. That's a coincidence," Gideon said. He furrowed his brow. He didn't believe in coincidences.

"What do you know about Jeoseung Saja?" Gideon asked absently.

"Not a lot. Um…generally a man…usually handsome… like a…grim reaper," he replied. "Why?"

Gideon smiled sadly. "I dream about one," he replied. George looked concerned. "He's Seong Min."

George breathed a sigh of relief. "Oh. That's natural. I mean…he's dead. He's your love's father. It makes sense. I wouldn't worry about it."

Gideon chuckled, but it still felt mournful. "You dream of him, too. He's visited your hotel room. He's talked to you about me. But he won't say my name. He just says…'he… him.' Same with Tracey…'she…her.'"

George cocked his head to the side. "Ayuh, I do. How?"

"He told me. In the car…on the way here."

———

Tracey poured coffee into an insulated mug and pushed the top on it. She walked casually toward the front door, pausing to straighten up the boots by the door. She opened the door and stepped out onto her front porch.

Her front porch. Goose Fields Cottage had become hers and Gideon's almost effortlessly. He had lost everything except the clothes on his back, his daughter, and his cat in the fire. And yet, the cottage was filled with him. His clean, masculine scent permeated the air. His new clothes had slowly appeared. Her mother's childhood bedroom had morphed into Cassie's childhood bedroom. Sphinx was a welcoming presence. She understood what Mark Twain meant by "A house is not a home without a cat."

The same was true of herself. She had arrived only with the few things she could fit into her old Impala, sadly now a total loss. Now, the cottage was arranged to her taste, and the furniture and décor she disliked had been removed and replaced. Artwork she liked covered the walls. And best of all, the sounds of the three of them, her, Gideon, and Cassie, filled the home. She loved the cottage because she loved the people and Tabby who shared it with her. She finally understood why she and her mother had never had a home. Judith Hyun had cut herself off from the world, including her daughter. They had loved one another, true, but they had not shared their lives. Perhaps Judith felt her depression was too heavy a load to share with anyone. But Tracey knew now that her mother had always been distant, at least since after Seong Min had died.

She could remember now happier days…well, one day, anyway. Christmas. And her memory was only a snapshot. They were around a Christmas tree, her, her parents, her aunt and uncle…and her halmeoni, grandma. Nothing more…just the feeling of home…like what she felt now.

"Trent," she called.

No one answered. The hair stood up on her arms. She turned and looked around. Trent was nowhere to be seen. "Trent!" she yelled, louder. She yelled again. "Trent! Where are you?"

No one answered.

———

Mr. Kingsford shook first Gideon's, then George's hand before taking a seat. "Hello, Gentlemen," he greeted them. "It's a pleasure to meet you. Dr. Spencer, I've read your thesis on forensic psychology. It is very insightful."

"Oh…um…thank you. Are you interested in law enforcement, Mr. Kingsford?" Gideon asked, scooting his chair back toward the table.

"As much as any businessman, I suppose," Mr. Kingsford said with a smile.

Their meals were brought immediately. Mr. Kingsford smiled and said, "Enjoy your meal. We'll discuss Ms. Biacchi while we eat, if you don't mind. I do have another meeting at 10. But feel free to stay as long as you like after I leave."

Gideon cut into his steak and took a bite. It was delicious. He nodded. "Oh, we won't take much of your time, Mr. Kingsford. We found a recording device in a suspect's home labeled with the name 'Biacchi Systems, Inc.' It also had your residence in Beacon Hill listed on the label. We checked the business registry, and it wasn't registered."

"Hmmm. Yes, I'm not surprised. Lisa Biacchi was a member of my household staff…security. She lived on the premises. I do recall her starting a business on the side and asking permission to list the address. I checked, and permission was granted. She was a graduate of MIT, and it was a Tech business…apparently, she built and repaired computers and computer equipment…including recording devices. She left our employ 2 years ago. I believe she said she was getting married," Mr. Kingsford replied.

"You could have told us this over the phone, Mr. Kingsford…or had your HR department tell us. Why did you insist on meeting us here?" George asked, taking a bite of his steak as he spoke.

"Yes. That's true. But the thing is…I…I'm concerned. Lisa left under strange circumstances. I mean, she was behaving strangely…and when she left, something…a very valuable something...disappeared," the CEO said quietly.

"A valuable something?" Gideon asked.

"Yes. Very. A valuable...proprietary something. Belonging to Kingsford Systems. Not something we want the public to know is...missing."

"We can't promise that any items recovered won't be made public record, Mr. Kingsford," Gideon said indignantly.

"Yes, I am aware. I don't suppose it will matter when and if you find it, anyway, Dr. Spencer. We stole it, too...from you." Mr. Kingsford announced.

Gideon took a deep breath. "My forensic profiling program?"

Mr. Kingsford smiled coldly and nodded.

"I see. And...you bought it from..."

"Steve Unger."

"Scott's brother? Interesting," Gideon huffed. He pushed away his plate. "What does Lisa have to do with it?"

"I think she took it for you," Mr. Kingsford replied.

"Because she's obsessed with me?" Gideon scoffed. "So, she's dangerous?"

"No. She wasn't...isn't...her brother...well, he's a different story," the CEO advised. "He's...dangerous...as you say. She's just trying to mitigate the damage he causes. Truthfully, they're both psychopaths."

"What are you?" George interrupted.

"He's a psychopomp...and a sociopath," Gideon replied.

"Hmmm. Psychopomp? That's a first. But yes, I suppose most men of my stature are psychopomps. Life...at least the lives of others are...irrelevant. The road to success is paved in the bones of those who get us there. I suppose we could be seen as the one who escorts their souls to the afterlife, metaphorically."

"I mean it, literally, Mr. Kingsford. It's your fate. You just haven't met it yet," Gideon said, standing. "We won't keep you. You have another meeting. As for my program... well, it doesn't work. You stole nothing. I designed it to fail. At least that version." He paused as George stood. He shoved his hands into his pockets and smiled. "Have a good night, Mr. Kingsford." He turned and walked away. George hurried after him.

"What the hell just happened?" George asked him as he pulled off the dinner jacket and tie, handing them back to the Maître D'.

"I created a computer program that would revolutionize profiling with AI...while at Boston College. A version was stolen from the lab. I, however, didn't trust the security, so it was a dummy version. The real program...is...safe," Gideon acknowledged. "I sold it to his competitor...years ago.

"For how much?"

Gideon laughed. "$50 million."

"Where is it? The money, I mean..." George gasped. He was clearly stunned.

"I have it," Gideon guffawed.

"You have $50 million?"

"No. I have close to $110 million. I created other programs as well."

They walked out the door. George dug into his pocket for the valet parking ticket. He handed it to the valet. "Holy shit," he said as the valet grabbed their keys off the board and walked off to retrieve the Tahoe.

CHAPTER 20

Tracey tried to remember what she saw. There was that rock that looked like a whale. They went right at the fork on the trail, away from the lake. Up. They were climbing. Woods. All the trees looked alike. It was difficult to pick a landmark. The trees were thicker, harder to pass through...then they were on a bluff overlooking a cove. God, she wished she had explored more...maybe she'd have an idea of where she was now if she had. She stumbled.

Dom yanked her back to her feet and pulled her along. He had cuffed her hands together in front of her and had tethered a rope to her waist and his. He had put duct tape over her mouth, so she couldn't scream, though she desperately wanted to.

It was dark, and she was scared...no, terrified. What had happened to Trent? Was he okay? He was having a baby. God, she hoped he was okay. She'd called his name... and then...something struck her in the head from behind. She'd regained consciousness in the trunk of Dom's car. Her head hurt...and after the stumble, so did her knee. Dom was unrelenting. He pulled her along in silence. Suddenly, they were in a clearing, and there was a cabin in front of them.

The strange woman she'd met at Shaw's came out of the door and onto the porch. "What have you done?" she admonished the silent deputy.

"I promised you'd be the one he married," Dom sneered, yanking on the rope and shoving Tracey to the ground. She fell. There was a dusting of snow, and the ground was cold and hard. It was so cold it burned the palms of her hands as she threw them, cuffed together, out in front of her to break her fall.

"You can't keep taking women he talks to," the woman scoffed.

"He doesn't just talk to her, Lisa. He's going to marry her." He knelt on one knee beside Tracey and yanked the duct tape off her mouth, taking skin with it. She cried out in pain. "Isn't that right?" he asked, smirking.

"We're already married," she admitted, looking him bravely in the eyes.

"Oh, Jesus," Lisa huffed. "Get her inside. I'll clean up her wounds."

He hauled her to her feet again before flinging her over his shoulder. He fireman carried her inside the cabin, which was clean and tidy inside. A fire burned in a woodstove. It was warm. But it was far from cozy, despite the attempts to make it so. There were pretty quilts and pillows on the sofa…a shag rug on the floor…curtains on the windows…and yet the cabin was more terrifying than the woods outside it. There were doors with huge padlocks on them…with barred windows in them…like some medieval jail cell doors. The windows of the cabin were barred, too, she noticed, now that Tracey could see better in the light inside. Dom carried her to one of the padlocked doors.

"Open it," he bellowed.

Lisa hurried past him and unlocked the padlock. She pulled open the door. The cell beyond the door was dark and colder than the room outside it. There was a cot with a quilt and a pillow inside. Nothing else. No table. No chair. Just the cot. Dom threw Tracey down on it. She fell hard on it, like a sack of potatoes. It knocked the air out of her lungs. Her head felt like it might explode as the pain shot through her. She cried out, unable to stifle the gasp.

He untied the rope from around her waist but left her hands cuffed.

"She'll be fine," he said gruffly. "I didn't hit her that hard. Clean her up and leave her be."

The woman shook her head and pushed into the room past Dom. She was carrying a first aid kit. She knelt beside the cot and pulled Tracey to a seated position. "You'll be okay, Tracey," she said coldly. "Women like you always are."

"Women like me? What does that mean? What am I like?" She wanted to know more…anything. Why had they brought her here? Why were they doing this? Who were they, really? Just get her to talk to you, Tracey thought frantically.

"You know…pretty…get everything you ever want," Lisa smirked.

In pain and fear, Tracey half-laughed and half-cried. "I've never had anything until now. I've been alone most of my life. I only had dreams. Now that my dreams have finally come true, a woman like you wants to take it from me," she sobbed.

Lisa glared at Tracey as she cleaned up and bandaged the scrapes and bruises on Tracey's knees. "You don't know anything about me," she hissed.

"True. And likewise," Tracey retorted. She didn't care anymore. She wanted the odious woman to leave. She wanted them to shut that massive wooden door with the small, barred window. She wanted them to lock her in this dark, cramped room…as long as she was alone. She needed to sleep. She needed to dream.

Lisa finished with her knees and grabbed her hands. "These abrasions just need cleaning," she said roughly, washing the scraped palms. Tracey did her best not to flinch.

Lisa stood and picked up the first aid kit. She turned and walked out the door. She slammed the door shut with Tracey inside and glared at her through the little window, as sounds of the lock being slipped into the latch and slammed closed pierced the quiet. Then she was gone, and only the light from the room outside was visible through the little window and bars. Tracey cried quietly as she lay back on the cot. She closed her eyes and prayed for sleep and that he was asleep, too.

Gideon found himself walking along the shoreline of Sebec Lake. But it wasn't a spring day, as it was usually in his dreams. It was winter. There was snow. And the trees were bare.

"Gideon!" came Tracey's voice from far away. It was carried on the wind. "Gideon! Help me!"

He whirled in a circle, looking for her, but there was no one…just the lake, the naked trees, and him. "Tracey!" he yelled.

"I'm here," came the voice, but he couldn't see her and couldn't tell where her voice was coming from.

"Where? Where are you?" he called, panic starting to set in.

"Up," came the response. "Past the rock that looks like a whale."

Orca Rock. Okay, he knew where that was.

"A cabin…up…They…took me."

Then he was there. Eagle Nest Lodge to the west. Sebec Lake to the south. The hunting cabin where he'd first met Scott when he was 13, where he'd had the bad potato salad that caused his food poisoning. He'd been the only one to eat it. Then he'd dreamt of Tracey for the first time, before they had ever met in real life. She had handed him her friendship bracelet in that first dream. He had awakened to find it in his hand for real. He had not dreamt of her again until after she had shown up at MIT for a tour 10 years ago. He had recognized her from his dream then, but, having been at a loss to explain it, he'd not said anything.

He went into the cabin. Tracey was locked in a cell, and he couldn't free her. She smiled sadly through the bars on a little window in the door. "Here," she said, passing her love knot bracelet he'd just bought her through the bars. He took it and shoved it into his jacket pocket.

"I'm coming to get you, Baby. I'm coming," he promised.

He sat bolt upright, gasping for air. He was in the dark vehicle. He turned and looked at George, who was driving. "Dom and Lisa have Tracey," he said.

George looked at him. "You were dreaming, Kiddo. It was just a dream," he reassured Gideon. But Gideon knew better. He shook his head.

"No, George. Tracey and I...our dreams...we're together in our dreams...for real. That's why we're so sure about us. We've been sharing dreams for years. We've known each other in our dreams for years."

George chuckled. Of course, he did. Why would he believe Gideon?

"You have to believe me, George. They have her,"

he swore earnestly, grabbing the older man's arm. George's phone rang at that moment. He shook off Gideon's hand and picked up the phone. "Hello, Officer Forrest," he said, placing the call on speaker.

"I...I lost her," Trent's voice groaned over the speaker. "I was...standing on the porch...and something struck me from behind...and I woke up in the barn. Cal...found me. Tracey's gone."

George stared at Gideon. Gideon sobbed and nodded, holding George's gaze.

———

Tracey sputtered and gasped as the cold water drenched her face and hair. She opened her eyes to blinding pain. Lisa stepped closer, throwing the now-empty bucket onto the floor.

"Wake up," she growled through gritted teeth at Tracey, who shivered and sat up on the hard cot.

"Why?" Tracey sobbed, barely able to breathe from the cold water and pain.

"You called his name," Lisa spat at her. "You have no right."

"He's my husband. I have every right. I am the only one with the right," she retorted, still gasping for breath. She straightened her spine and lifted her chin. "He didn't even know who you were. He had to look you up in a yearbook to figure it out," she declared defiantly. "He knew me the second he saw me. After 9 years...when we'd only spent a single day together. He called me by name. Ask your brother. He was there." This bitch didn't need to know about the dreams or that Gideon had heard her. He was coming to get her now. All she had to do was hold on.

Lisa turned bright red. Her chest heaved as she fought the angry outburst she so obviously wanted to have. She gave in to her baser desires. The smack stung Tracey's face. Though her cheek was numbed by the cold, her face burned from the strike. She gasped in pain again, but she did not cry. She simply sat back up straight and looked at Lisa.

"Why would he remember you, Lisa? He only did for you what he would have done for anyone. You weren't special. In fact, you were kind of pathetic. A little cold water, and you couldn't fight back." The words were harsh. And Tracey would never have said them if Lisa weren't a complete psychopath. It was probably not smart to challenge Lisa, but Tracey couldn't let her see that she was afraid. That would never do. If Lisa saw fear, she'd have won.

Lisa reared back to smack her again, but Dom's voice rang out. "Enough!" he yelled from outside the cell somewhere. "He won't pay if she's damaged."

Ransom? They took her for ransom? No one knew about the money.

CHAPTER 21

Gideon rushed into the ER exam room, shoving the curtain aside with far more exertion than necessary. Trent was sitting up on the exam table. Dr. Burns was stitching up the gash on the back of his head behind his right ear.

"You okay?" Gideon blurted.

"I'm okay. Just a superficial cut," Trent answered. "I'm so…sorry. I…I failed."

Gideon shook his head and put his hand on Trent's shoulder. "Don't. You've been great, Trent. The important thing is that you're okay and to get her back. Can you tell me anything?"

"No. I didn't see anything out of the ordinary before I was hit. I…I thought I heard something, but it was from the barn, and I was hit from behind while looking toward the barn. It was probably just the sheep," Trent bemoaned. He shook his head as the doctor cut the twine, having finished the stitches. "God…I'm so sorry. If it were Tricia…I'd be ready to kill me."

Gideon smiled sadly. "What good would that do, Trent?" he asked earnestly. He knew Trent hadn't let this happen intentionally. A sound from the barn before he'd been struck from behind? Had Dom and Lisa worked together to kidnap Tracey? Phillip Kingsford seemed to have believed that Dom was the one directing Lisa.

Gideon turned and pulled his phone out of his pocket. He called Scott Unger's cell this time. He wanted answers now.

"Hey," Scott answered on the second ring. "Did you find Ms. Biacchi?"

"Steve stole my thumb drive, Scott," he said into the phone. "Did you know?"

"What?" his longtime best friend countered. "Says who?"

"Phillip Kingsford, IV."

"That asshole? He's a thief. And he's a liar," Scott insisted.

"I'm aware, but he wasn't lying about this. Steve stole it and sold it to him, and Dom and Lisa stole it from Kingsford. Fortunately, it's a dummy. I sold the real program to Law Enforcement Solutions, Inc. Kingsford Tech announced the release of their version just after LES did. Only the Kingsford version never worked properly...because I coded in bugs. Steve opened a Swiss bank account the day before the announcement."

Scott was silent for a moment. "I don't know anything about it, Gideon. I swear."

"I believe you," Gideon replied. He could hear it in Scott's voice. He remembered how the Ungers treated Scott... like the outsider. Even now, he had been relegated to running the family foundation instead of working at the corporate level at Unger Communications, a cable and internet provider, where his brother and sisters worked. That was a bit of an understatement. Unger Communications was the largest cable and internet provider in the Northeast and the fastest-growing nationwide.

Scott was the offspring of his older siblings' nanny. James Unger, Scott's father, had had an affair with her. Beatrice

Thomas-Unger, James's first wife, demanded a divorce. James then married Clarissa...the nanny...and Scott's mother. That marriage also ended in divorce when James again dallied with a younger, more buxom woman. Scott's father was now on his fifth marriage. His 3 younger siblings, by subsequent wives, did not suffer the same disdain he did from the elder Unger offspring, in that they were all girls...and had no interest in the business. They were instead famous for their social media presence and partying.

Steven Edward Unger was ambitious. He wanted to expand their business. He'd long wanted to partner with Kingsford Technologies. Gideon could see him taking any opportunity to make that relationship happen. And he could see Scott being left completely out of the loop.

"Does Steve have any connection to Lisa Biacchi or Dominic Moretti?" he asked after a deep cleansing breath.

"Um...not that I know of off the top of my head...other than Lisa's being a scholarship recipient, like I already told you. But let me look again," Scott answered softly. Gideon heard the clicks on Scott's computer keyboard.

"Wait...did you say Dominic Moretti? There's no Dominic, but there was a Regina Moretti. Um...She's retired from Unger Communications. She...worked out of Trenton. Looks like she retired 15 years ago, though."

"Dom's mother is named Regina. Would Steve have any direct contact with her?"

"Well, yeah. She retired on disability after being hurt on the job. Steve was the head of HR at the time, and he handled her case personally."

"I need to talk to her. Now. They have Tracey," Gideon confided.

Scott quickly texted him the information he had on Regina Moretti.

————

Tracey shivered and curled herself into a fetal position on the cot. She hugged her knees, and her teeth chattered. She was wet, and the cell in which Dom and Lisa had her locked was dark and cold. She was terrified. But she had to believe Gideon was coming to get her. He'd told her he would in the dream. She had long since come to believe that even in her dreams, he was real. He'd heard her calling to him, even though she couldn't find their spot on the lake. He'd heard her and had called back to her that he was coming.

Dom's voice boomed from the cabin outside the cell. "The statie? I knocked him out. He heard an animal out in the barn and looked away to see if it was a threat. He'll live, but he'll have one hell of a headache."

A man's voice, one Tracey did not recognize, answered, "As long as the girlfriend is okay…at least until we get the ransom. I can't believe that son of a bitch switched out that program. The best laid plans…"

"Help," Tracey called out.

There was the sound of footsteps crossing the wood floors of the cabin. A heavy fist pounded on the cell door. "Quiet, Tracey. It won't be long now. Once he pays, we'll let you go," Dom said wickedly. He even laughed after he said it. If Dom had his way, she'd never leave this cabin alive.

"Please, Dom. Let me go," she cried.

"Sorry, Tracey. You walked into a shit show. We'd planned on taking the kid. You can be thankful we took you instead, at least," he cackled.

Then his footsteps retreated, and the cabin fell quiet

again.

Tracey turned her face to the meager pillow and cried herself to sleep again.

———

Gideon pushed past Harry Westin, the deputy on duty at the sheriff's office. George followed, nearly unable to keep up.

Harry was older than George, a retired Chicago police officer, who had moved to Maine three years back because he loved the outdoors and the hunting the area offered. He worked mainly nights because he enjoyed the quiet and peace, but wanted a paycheck to supplement his pension, because he had three ex-wives and four kids in college still.

"Deputy Spencer, Detective Davison," Harry greeted them. "You need somethin'?"

Gideon ignored him. George frowned. "He's not in a good place," George confided.

Harry nodded. "I heard. Ralph has it under control. You need to stay out of it, Son."

"Not happening," Gideon grumbled. "She's my wife."

Harry Westin's eyebrow rose. "Ralph and the boys will find her."

Gideon rummaged through his desk. He found the keys he was searching for. "Yeah, but I know where she is," he grumbled.

"What?" Harry countered. Gideon shoved the keys into his pocket and walked back out the door. "What did he say?" Harry asked George.

George shrugged and followed his nephew-in-law.

"What are the keys to?" he called to Gideon's quickly retreating back.

"Eagle Nest Lodge," Gideon replied.

"Eagle Nest Lodge?" George queried, standing in front of the Tahoe.

"It's a lodge on a bluff overlooking the north bank of Sebec Lake. It's owned by the Ungers," Gideon said. "That's how Scott and I got to know each other. They'd spend summers out here. There are a few remote cabins on the property as well. Dom has Tracey at the old hunting cabin a few miles off in the woods from the lodge."

"How do you know that, Gideon? For certain? I mean, I get you believe this dream thing, but..." George argued.

Gideon sighed. "When we left, what bracelet did Tracey have on her wrist?"

"What?"

"Her bracelet?" Gideon insisted.

"Um...I think it was the one you bought her the other day...the Korean knot one," George responded.

"She had it? Not me?"

"Yes, of course," George affirmed.

Gideon reached into his pocket, pulled the bracelet out, and held it up. "I believe the dream thing. I'm certain."

George's mouth fell open. He nodded and got into the passenger side of the SUV, letting Gideon drive this time.

As Gideon drove, he handed George his phone. "Call that number for me, please," he asked the older man. "On speaker," Gideon requested. He was laser-focused. If Gideon had reminded George of Shawn before, now it would be irrefutable. As a car approached them from the opposite direction, Gideon even looked like Shawn. It was an eerie optical illusion...as if Shawn's face were projected over Gideon's by the oncoming car's headlights.

"Shawn?" George whispered, staring at Gideon. Then the effect vanished as the car disappeared on the road behind them, and Gideon was Gideon again.

"What?" Gideon asked, turning to look at George.

"Sorry...nothing," he said, shaking his head. He made the call. It was close to 2 a.m. George had no idea who he was calling, but the woman's voice was strangely familiar when she sleepily answered.

"Somebody better be dead," she hacked and coughed into the receiver.

"Mrs. Moretti," Gideon said, "Sorry to wake you. My name is Gideon Spencer..."

"Oh, is Dom okay?"

"No. He most assuredly is not okay. He's kidnapped my wife, demanding I marry Lisa Biacchi instead, and wants 4 million dollars of my money," Gideon sneered.

"Oh...oh, dear," Regina Moretti responded.

George suddenly knew why her voice was so familiar. The night Shawn had died...the man who had shot him...his wife was on the phone now, just as she had been that night.

"Mrs. Moretti? Joey...Moretti..." he stammered in shock.

"Who are you?" the woman demanded.

George sighed. "George Davison," he huffed. Deputy Spencer is my...niece's husband. Seong Min Hyun...was her father...and my partner."

"Oh...well...that's...just perfect," the woman sobbed. "I should have known Dom would pay the price for his father's mistakes."

"Mistake?" George scoffed. "Joey killed Seong Min. He killed a police officer in the commission of a felony...and then committed suicide by cop. I had to...I had to shoot him, knowing I was giving him his way out of...paying for his crime," George cried.

Gideon shook his head. "Great. So, we're all caught up on the players in this little drama," he interjected. "I know where he is. I know where Tracey is being held. Did you put Dom in contact with Steve Unger? Is he behind this?"

"That little weasel? He came to me looking for Dom. I told Dom to stay away from that guy. But he didn't listen."

The pain was excruciating, even in sleep. Tracey felt like she was floating somewhere between consciousness and nothing. It wasn't sleep exactly, but it was dreamlike, and therein lay her hope. Maybe Gideon could reach her here, in that state. "Gideon," she moaned, curling into a ball on the hard, cold, and wet cot. She floated in a sea of black that might have been the cell Dom, Lisa, and the nameless man had her locked up in, though it seemed bigger, infinite even, than the small cell.

She cried.

"Tracey," came her mother's voice out of the darkness. "You're okay. I promise."

"Mama," she exclaimed, reaching out, only to have the cuffs around her wrists bite hard into her as the chain caught on the metal rung of the cot through which Dom had threaded the cuffs the last time he'd come into the cell to torture her mind.

"Here," he said, smirking as he'd unlocked the right cuff, only to thread the chain through the rung of the cot, which was bolted to the floor, and re-cuff her immediately. "Should you accept the illusion that you have any freedom,

Miss Hyun, let me disillusion you. Or do you prefer Mrs. Spencer? Do you think he loves and respects you? You don't even know him!" he spat. "You don't know who he really is… what he has."

"The money? Sorry to disappoint you, but he's told me. He's added me to his accounts. I have full access to it. All of it."

"All $50 million?" Dom scoffed.

She smiled wickedly. "That's cute. You only know about $50 million."

He had slammed the door, cursing her.

Now, in this twilight, she was afraid the fear would finally win, but her mother's voice called out to her, and she swallowed the fear again.

"You're doing great, Baby. Keep it up," Judith said, materializing on the cot, sitting beside her.

"You lied to me, Mama," Tracey cried.

"Yes. I did. And I can't take it back. I couldn't…I couldn't live without him, Baby. You were the only thing that kept me holding on. I held on as long as I could," her mother cried.

"Why did you tell me he died when I was a baby?"

"Because if you didn't remember him, you wouldn't miss him like I did."

"Do you know what kind of curse that put on him?" Tracey implored.

"Yes. Now. But then…all I could think was that he was gone, and I couldn't cope." Judith sighed. "He's free again, Baby. Because of you. If only I were."

From the darkness, Tracey heard her mother's name being called. "Judith. Where are you, Judy?"

A bright light pierced the darkness, and a woman's hand reached out from the inky black. She was an older version of Judy.

"Come," she said to her daughter. "It's almost over. Come into the light. He's here now."

Tracey closed her eyes against the brightness of the light. She turned and buried her face in the wet pillow to protect her eyes.

She was aware of the sound of wood splintering as something heavy crashed into the cabin outside the dark cell. There was shouting. There were shots. And then the lock was being forced from the door. Then it swung open.

"Tracey!" Gideon shouted, rushing to her and cutting the chain that held her to the cot. She flung herself into his arms.

"Are you real?" she sobbed uncontrollably.

"I'm always real, my love. Always." Then he put her bracelet back onto her wrist and hugged her close to him.

———

Tracey woke up to the beeping of the hospital monitor. Her head still ached, but it was no longer excruciating. She turned to see Gideon, sleeping in the chair beside her hospital bed.

"Gideon," she whispered hoarsely, squeezing his hand, which was in hers.

He roused and leaned forward, smiling. "Hey, Baby," he greeted her. "You're awake. Thank God."

"What happened?" she croaked.

"George and I came to get you. That's all."

"It's not," she said. She could see it in his eyes.

He was tearing up. "I...He came at us. He raised his

weapon. I had to shoot. I shot Dom. He's dead," he said, his lip quivering.

"Lisa?" she asked.

"She's in custody, along with Steve Unger. She admitted to burning down the trailer, but she made sure the cat was out and that no one was home. She says that Dom did the killing. Evidence still points to her, but…she's not well… mentally, I mean. And she hasn't been for a long time. She'll be committed. Dom started out trying to protect her, I think. Then he just got…greedy. Steve convinced him he could get some of our money."

"Your money," she corrected him.

"No. Our money. Anyway, Steve…well, he's old New England money. He'll get a slap on the hand, no doubt. The others, Hailey Burns and Grace Kemp, were being held in the other cells in the cabin. They are safe…if a little worse for the wear. They've been through a terrible ordeal," he explained. "I'm so sorry, Baby. I didn't protect you."

"You came to get me, Honey," she sighed. "Nobody can be with someone every second of the day. I knew you'd come."

CHAPTER 22

Gideon stood under the floral arch at the far end of the greenhouse beside Isaac, who insisted on standing with the use of a crutch. Cal and Trent stood behind Isaac as groomsmen.

Nettie, Janey, and Hana Jin had cleaned and decorated the old greenhouse until it sparkled like crystal in the autumn sunset. The florist, Dennis Hampton, had outdone himself with maple leaves in brilliant reds and yellows arranged with Queen Anne's Lace and sunflowers, a rustic touch that fit the farm venue perfectly.

The music started, and Janey, followed by Tricia Forrest, and finally Gigi, walked slowly down the aisle in simple yellow gowns. Cassie carried a basket of red rose petals and was dressed in her own white gown, because it was her wedding, too. Sam, in a little tuxedo, walked beside Cassie, holding a little white satin pillow bearing the wedding rings. Tracey, on George's arm, was breathtaking in Hana's hanbok.

As his bride's uncle walked her down the aisle to him, Gideon just tried to breathe.

He felt the hand on his shoulder and heard the whisper in his ear. "I knew you were the one. Make each other happy," the voice of Seong Min said. Then the sensation vanished. Gideon smiled. He knew somehow that the dreams would stop. They were living it now. There was no more need. They were together now, forever. Every moment was the dream. And they would share this reality for the rest of their lives together.

George winked at him as he and Tracey reached the makeshift altar. He offered his niece's hand to her groom. Gideon stepped forward and took Tracey's hand into his own. They exchanged their wedding vows again with all their family and friends as witnesses to their everlasting love for one another.

Mr. Hancock once again pronounced Gideon and Tracey as man and wife. Gideon sealed it with a sweet kiss on Tracey's perfect mouth. They turned to face everyone as the greenhouse filled with applause.

The rows of chairs were quickly replaced with tables, and the altar became a dance floor while Gideon, Tracey, and Cassie posed for photos. The guests were offered appetizers and drinks on the lawn overlooking the pasture and the Christmas tree farm, while the greenhouse was swiftly transformed from chapel to banquet hall.

The DJ started playing his set as Nettie and Tom, George and Hana Jin, and the rest of the wedding party welcomed the guests back inside the greenhouse before dinner.

"This is amazing, Nettie," Gretchen Banks, the clerk at the Stop Buy convenience store, whom Tracey had met on that first rainy night in Piscataquis County, said, shaking Gideon's mother's hand. "My Barbie is getting married in the spring. We'd love to look at some dates when you have the time."

"Oh, of course, Gretchen. Call Janey on Monday to set up an appointment. We'll be offering a wide range of services from the complete wedding to a more do-it-out yourself package. I'm sure we'll be able to find a package that meets your needs and budget," Nettie replied with an excited smile. When Gretchen and her husband, Vern Banks, had moved along to their table, she did an excited little jig and gave Janey a thumbs-up across the greenhouse.

Gideon smiled to see his mother so happy.

Tracey took his arm, and together they entered the greenhouse as the DJ introduced them as Mr. and Mrs. Gideon Spencer. They took to the dance floor as "*In Dreams*" by Roy Orbison played. Gideon held Tracey in his arms. She had removed the hanbok and was wearing the slip dress, now... and she was beautiful. "I love you, Tracey," he whispered.

"I love you, too," she replied.

The song ended, and "*We Are Family*" started. Cassie ran onto the dance floor. Gideon swung her up into his arms. Tracey grabbed her hand, and the three of them continued to dance as the rest of the family, George and Hana Jin included, joined them on the dance floor.

———

The party broke up sometime after midnight. Nettie and Tom took Cassie for the night, though truth be told, she had fallen asleep around 9 pm. Tom had taken her back to the house alone because Nettie wanted to supervise everything. Three more couples after Gretchen had requested appointments, and she wanted to show she was capable. Poor Isaac and his leg lasted only until 10, when he took Sam and Vivian back to the house to take over for Tom.

Gideon and Tracey left around 11:30.

They were spending the night at Goose Fields Cottage, but were leaving the next day, with Cassie, for a "family" honeymoon in Disney World.

But for tonight, they were alone. Cal and Gigi were staying at Isaac and Janey's.

Gideon picked Tracey up into his arms and kissed her deeply as he stepped across the threshold of their cozy little home. She let herself melt into his kiss. This was the life she had always dreamt of. She was happy…at last.

Lacynda Mathes is a graduate of Radford University in Radford, VA. She holds a B.A. in English.

She is originally from Oak Grove, VA, in Westmoreland County near Colonial Beach. She graduated from Washington and Lee High School, Montross, VA, in 1986. She attended Randolph-Macon College, studied abroad at Wroxton College in Oxfordshire, England, and ultimately transferred to Radford University, where she completed her degree.

She currently resides in Sterling, IL, with her husband. She is the mother to their teenage sons, the eldest with special needs, who has been diagnosed with Lennox Gestaut Syndrome, a catastrophic childhood epilepsy, and severe autism.